DEADLY EXPOSURE

A ROMANTIC SUSPENSE NOVEL

CARA PUTMAN

D1319197

Find rest, O my soul, in God alone; my hope comes from Him. He alone is my rock and my salvation; He is my fortress, I will not be shaken.
—*Psalms* 62:5-6

To Colleen Coble.

When we met in April 2005, I couldn't imagine the friendship God had in store for us. Thank you so much for taking my dream and breathing life into it. You truly were the midwife for this book. I am honored to count you as a friend and mentor.

ACKNOWLEDGMENTS

A book isn't written in a vacuum. Many thanks to Sabrina Butcher, who read this book in each of its iterations, and to Gina Conroy and Sabrina who read the final draft under a crazy deadline. You gals pushed me to make this book better. Thanks to Rachel Allen, Virgene Putman and Rhonda Putman for watching my kids as I raced to finish this book against a tight deadline.

Thanks to Eric for always believing I could do this, to Abigail and Jonathan for being so proud of their mommy. Thanks to Krista Stroever, my editor, for taking a risk on this writer. And to Karen Solem for believing I could do this.

And for this updated edition, thanks to my son Jonathan for helping me format the book.

1

Dani Richards barely noticed where the usher pointed as she turned to take Aunt Jayne's arm but groped emptiness. Dani spun in a circle, searching for her. "Aunt Jayne?"

"She went that way, ma'am."

Dani nodded at the usher and hurried across the plush red carpet toward the boxes. She slipped into their box, but it remained empty. Then she heard a raised voice from the adjoining box. She darted to it, parted the curtain and pushed through. Aunt Jayne relaxed next to a young woman whose stiff back and chin pointed high made it clear she was trying to avoid eye contact. "There you are. You scared me to death, Aunt Jayne."

"No need to worry. I looked for our seats and found this lovely young lady instead."

"You don't belong here." The woman looked from Dani to her aunt, emerald eyes flashing. Her regal bearing sagged with a hint of disappointment. She glanced beyond Dani into the emptying foyer.

Aunt Jayne patted her hand. "Don't worry. Your young man will join you. You're too lovely to miss."

Dani examined the woman more closely, wondering why she seemed so familiar. In her job as a reporter, she worked with too many people to count in an average week, but this woman tugged at her memory. "Have we met before?"

"Please leave." With a quick twist of her wrist the woman glanced at her watch.

"Sorry for the interruption. Come on, Aunt Jayne. *Cats* starts any minute." Together they reentered the foyer and slipped up the stairs to the right box. Dani released a deep breath, determined to enjoy every moment of the evening. After the latest trial she'd covered on her crime beat for Channel 17, she'd earned the reprieve. Her aunt deserved her full attention on a night when the cloud of Alzheimer's had slipped away, even fleetingly.

Aunt Jayne sank into her seat and smiled. "Thank you for bringing me, dear. It's so nice to have you in town again."

Dani settled beside her in a maroon seat as the orchestra crescendoed into the opening notes of the musical, prepared to relish each moment. She'd spent the five years since graduation working her way through the ranks of broadcast journalism, moving from Cheyenne to Des Moines to St. Louis. She'd given it all up to move to Lincoln for Aunt Jayne. Her mom believed she'd lost her mind, and her dad tried to convince her to take a job at his station in Chicago each time they talked.

Lincoln had been lonely, especially when Aunt Jayne's bad days outnumbered the good. She'd wanted to dance when she reached Peaceful Estates and found Aunt Jayne alert and excited. A sliver remained of the woman Dani remembered from summers spent in Lincoln. If only she reappeared more often.

The curtain rose, and Dani leaned into the railing. She glanced at the neighboring box, but couldn't see more than outlines in the darkness. The opening song began, and her attention focused completely on the stage covered by a large set that resembled a junkyard. The actors stretched and danced as they mimicked cats and sang. The scenes flew by, and too soon the curtain sank for intermission.

Dani shifted against the seat and straightened. Renee Thomas. That was the woman's name. She'd interviewed the grad student for a story on promising research at the university. Though Renee had been formal and distant tonight, she'd been much friendlier and relaxed during the interview. Odd, since people tended to freeze in that setting. She'd practically glowed as she discussed the research, something about protecting the food supply from terrorist attacks. Dani had worked with her to describe the research in layman's terms.

Aunt Jayne tapped Dani's arm lightly. Dani smiled. "Are you okay? Need a break from sitting?"

"Maybe we should hunt for the story. Surely it's hiding somewhere." Aunt Jayne looked at her, amusement glowing in her eyes.

"There's a loose plot, keep watch." Dani stretched in her seat and her gaze slid into the box to her right. Renee sat motionless. She studied the woman, remembering the edge of worry that marred her expression. Renee had remained alone after all. "Let's stretch our legs a bit."

They stepped into the wide hallway. Dani looked around, hoping tonight wouldn't be the time she ran into the only person she'd allowed to break her heart. Caleb Jamison. The thought of him made her emotions spiral into a tornado of anger and hurt. She looked over her shoulder, afraid he'd appear like some horror-movie ghoul. Wished she could wipe her memory of him.

"Aunt Jayne, let's step up here. I interviewed your new friend last week. Maybe she'd like to join us."

Dani approached the neighboring box. She knocked on the doorframe, parted the curtain and entered the woman's box. A spicy fragrance tinged the air.

"Renee?" Dani waited a moment. The woman never turned. The seconds ticked by. "Are you enjoying the show? Andrew Lloyd Webber is a genius."

Renee remained silent. Dani stepped closer. One part of her mind began to insist she leave. Now.

Dani tapped Renee on the shoulder. Her skin felt cool. With quick steps she circled the seat and stood in front of Renee. Dani looked down, looking for a flash of recognition. Instead, Renee's gaze remained fixed, a horrible grimace pasted to her face. The emerald scarf wound tight around her neck in contrast to the way it floated earlier.

She sucked in a breath and willed herself to remain calm. Between the tightness of the scarf and the bruise lying under the woman's jaw, Dani's instinct jumped to murder. Bile rose in her throat. She put a hand over her mouth and swallowed.

This couldn't be happening again. Images of her college roommate's distorted features floated in front of Renee's. She'd been too late then. She couldn't be now. Dani rushed into the hall, fumbled for the cell phone in her evening bag and dialed 911. No service. She thrust the phone back into her purse. "Somebody call 911. There's a medical emergency. Does anyone know CPR?"

She didn't wait for an answer but ran back into the box. She sensed someone behind her. and turned to find Aunt Jayne. She pulled her attention back to Renee, and tried to ease her to the floor, struggling under the leaden weight.

Please don't let it be too late.

Concerned faces peered into Dani's from around the curtain. A well-dressed gentleman slipped into the box. He eased Renee the rest of the way to the floor, then loosened the scarf. He checked the woman's neck for a pulse. Dani watched him silently tick the seconds off his watch for an eternal moment. He shook his head and glanced at her. "It's too late."

Dani shuddered. She rose to her feet and took Aunt Jayne by the arm. "Let's get you back to our seats where you can be comfortable." A couple minutes later, Dani stood in the foyer. She took a step toward Renee's box, then turned back to her own. Aunt Jayne seemed fine, but Dani hesitated.

The news director would expect a complete report. She'd found the body, so she'd own the story from this moment. Somehow she'd balance that with caring for Aunt Jayne until she was back in her suite at Peaceful Estates. Interview questions ran through her mind. Someone had to have seen something.

"Ma'am, you have to stay until the police arrive." A tenor voice tickled her ear.

Dani jumped back against the wall. She turned toward the sound. An usher had invaded her space and her gaze met a fishy stare.

"You're a reporter with Channel 17, right?" He slid a half step back and licked his lips. "They...the police, I mean, should be here soon. They'll want to talk to you. You found the body."

She stepped to the side, unable to bear his proximity. "I promise I won't leave before the police arrive."

"Maybe I should clear the box." His gaze darted around the small area.

"It's a little late for that. Quite a few people have moved in and out already."

"Still, there must be something. They never told us what to do in a situation like this." Beads of sweat pooled on his brow as he twisted the top button of his shirt open. Angry uncertainty flashed across his face.

Dani leaned farther into the wall. "Are you okay? I'd be happy to get help."

"I'm fine." With a parting glare and tug at his collar, he turned on his heel and headed down the hall.

Dani watched him disappear, and then turned to the box. A security guard huffed up the stairs. A couple followed him. The man, tall and trim with a long stride, caught her eye. The woman held his arm and managed to keep up without looking rushed. Every brown piece of hair was in place, and her blue cocktail dress perfectly fit her athletic form. The man looked at her. Dani froze. One look in Caleb Jamison's face, and she reverted to the teenager head over heels for the star football player. The teenager who couldn't say no. The teenager who ached when he stopped seeing her. Stopped calling. Stopped caring.

The ice disappeared in a flash of anger. Her hands trembled. Her stomach clenched at the thought of his smug, self-satisfied face. She couldn't go back there. The echo of their baby's cries as she was given to others jarred Dani's mind. Caleb had abandoned her long before the birth. Yet here he was, cocky smile and all. He took a step toward her, and Dani escaped into the box.

2

Dani blinked to adjust to the dim lighting and pull her attention back from the nightmare of her past. The curtains brushed against her back, but she refused to turn and see who was there. *Note to self: don't run into a closed room when trying to avoid someone.* Several people filled the box. She worked her way toward a young coed.

A hand gripped her arm. Even though she knew it was Caleb, she jumped.

"Dani, we need to talk." His voice reached deep inside her. She stiffened. "But it'll wait. Right now you need to get out of this box. Wait for me in the lobby."

"Let go of me." Dani hissed and tried to shake free.

"I will when you start to obey."

"That worked so well for me last time." She snorted, stepping back. "Excuse me. I have a job to do."

She turned and ignored his soft chuckle. She didn't even want to know what amused him. She could imagine. None of the options merited turning around.

"Everyone out." Caleb's voice sank lower and easily filled the small space.

Dani kept her back to him as the crowd dispersed along with her interviews. She spun on her heel and followed everyone to the foyer. A burly security guard moved to the top step. He crossed his arms and stood legs apart, a barrier to reentry.

Caleb directed the group toward a small room, acting every bit the police officer. How could the young man who'd had no qualms about drinking underage and partying end up as an investigator with the Lincoln Police Department? And why was he with a beautiful woman?

Dani eased a coed and her date to the side. The twenty something young man looked like a player for the university's renowned football team. Their holey jeans and T-shirts stood out in the well-dressed crowd.

The girl clung to her date, wide-eyed. "This is wild. How could this happen here?"

"Yeah," the young man said. "I heard the excitement and rushed over. Wonder where her date is?" He tucked the girl under his arm.

Dani smiled at him. "Did either of you see her with anyone tonight?"

"Nope, but she wasn't dressed to be alone." He glanced toward the box. "Seems like a strange place for this to happen."

"Why would you say that? I've heard of stranger things."

"Maybe on *CSI*. But the theater is packed. Not a place I'd pick."

Dani shook her head. "Maybe not. Here's my card. If either of you think of anything, call."

She stepped back as Caleb waved the couple into the room. She scanned the foyer looking for others to talk to. No way was she stepping into a small space with him. It didn't matter how many other people were there.

Dani headed to her box and left the curtain open so she could watch the lobby. Maybe she'd be able to talk to someone other than Caleb when the other cops arrived. Her toes tapped the wall in front of her as she sat next to Aunt Jayne, her mind racing with everything she should do. Her aunt reached across the empty seat and placed her hand on Dani's knee.

"It'll be okay, child. He can't hurt you anymore."

Based on the jolt of electricity that hit her each time she saw Caleb, Dani doubted anything would be okay until she returned home and left the madness. The faint sound of sirens pierced the night. The sound sharpened until it stopped altogether. Rotating blue and red lights reflected off the foyer's floor-to-ceiling windows. She braced herself for the whirlwind the next few minutes would bring. Especially after the police learned a reporter discovered the body.

Those left in the lobby pressed against the windows, watching the police vehicles. What on earth were they doing outside?

Finally, a man in a dark suit, probably a theater employee, marched up the broad staircase. He wiped a few strands of hair across the top of his head as he looked behind him. Several uniformed policemen trailed at a determined pace.

"This way, Officers." The man pointed toward the box with a jerk of one arm while he wiped his brow with the other. "We've never had anything like this happen before. Excuse me. I must announce the show won't continue." Without waiting for an answer, he hurried off, mumbling under his breath. He wrung his hands in despair like the White Rabbit from *Alice in Wonderland*.

Caleb walked toward the officers, his dark hair standing at odd angles, as if he'd raked his fingers through it. Dani slipped from the box to watch.

"Glad you guys could make it. The body's in that box."

Caleb stepped around the security guard and poked his head past the curtain. He turned to the guard. "Anyone else been in here since you arrived?"

"Nope. I've kept it cleared." He puffed out his chest. Caleb turned to his men. "Ford, see if there's anyone still around to interview." He turned to another officer. "Get the box taped off. Denimore and Westmont, I've got a room with several people for you to interview. It doesn't look like they know anything, but we can hope. Let's see if we can piece together what happened while we wait for the crime scene techs." Caleb squared his shoulders as his calm gaze landed on Dani. "I'll come talk to you in a few minutes." His voice was deeper than she remembered with a timbre that made her quiver even as her stomach clenched. "Where's your seat?" She nodded toward the open doorway. He considered her a moment, then turned away.

Dani fought relief. "My aunt is with me, and I really need to get her home. Can't we talk now?"

"You'll have to wait a few minutes. Besides, I doubt you'll leave until after we do. I'll be back as soon as I can." He didn't wait for an answer before turning his back. "Maybe Tricia can help."

Tricia? His sister? Was she the woman he'd brought? Her traitorous stomach eased at the thought that he hadn't brought a date after all. She stared at Caleb's back, hands clenched, and then turned as movement caught her eye.

"Hi, Dani." A young, willowy woman approached. "Remember me? Caleb's kid sister who wouldn't leave you two alone? How can I help?"

How could she forget? They'd even been friends. "Aunt Jayne's with me, and I'm sure she'd appreciate company."

Dani led Tricia to box B. In no time, Tricia and Aunt Jayne were chatting like old friends. Dani tried to ignore them in favor of the foyer and Renee's box.

"Everything okay, Dani?" Aunt Jayne's eyes reflected concern.

"It will be." As soon as she didn't have to see Caleb anymore. She eased into a plush chair to dig through her evening bag in her lap for her cellphone. Dani glanced at the screen and this time saw bars of service. She dialed the station.

"Hey, LeAnn. I need Andy pronto." Andy Garrison produced the ten o'clock news and demanded the details of any news event fifteen minutes ago.

"Hey, kid. Exciting night at the theater." Andy's raspy voice scratched her ear.

"You have no idea." Dani twisted the purse strap in her lap with restless fingers.

"The news of a body hit the scanner. You still there?"

"Yep. The police won't let me leave."

"Just tell 'em you're media. They'll be more than glad to see you go."

"Not this time." She squinted at the techs working in the victim's box.

"What happened? You didn't kill her. did you?" Andy's rapid questions made Dani smile.

"Of course I didn't kill her. But I found her."

"Okay." He quieted, and Dani imagined him processing the information. "You holding up?"

"I'm fine. This isn't the first time I've seen a body. Just the first time I've seen one first."

"What can you tell me?"

"I had a brief conversation with her before the show started." Dani walked Andy through the night. "Nobody heard or saw anything. And the police won't like the fact that so many people invaded the box. It'll make evidence collection a nightmare."

"Hmm." Rapid-fire tapping on a keyboard echoed in the background. "As soon as the police let you go, find our truck. It should be there now. If the police harass you, give me a call. We'll get the station's attorney there ASAP."

Dani fiddled with a knot in her purse strap. If she did her job right, the attorney wouldn't be necessary. "I'll keep you posted." "Talk to people and make sure you connect with Logan. We've got a story to prepare."

Dani closed her phone, returned it to her purse and looked toward the other box. She rubbed the back of her neck. How could she take care of Aunt Jayne and deliver the story Andy expected? So much for a night off.

Investigators bent over the body in the taped-off box. A bright flash lit the scene as one photographed it. Another scribbled in a notebook. She wanted to look over his shoulder, see what required careful notes.

Caleb stood in the corner and anchored the controlled chaos. He looked even better than he had as an eighteen-year-old kid, and that thought rankled. Maybe if he wasn't so jaw-dropping, she'd have moved on.

No, she couldn't move on because of the lines they'd crossed. Color flooded her cheeks at the memory of what she'd willingly given him. And then he'd left. Without a backward glance. She'd prayed he'd call, show any indication he remembered her. Then she'd spent years trying to forget and move on. With one glance, all of that was swept aside. The emptiness she'd fought flooded back in. She wrapped her arms around her stomach and doubled over, fighting memories of the baby being ripped from her arms. Did the baby have his green eyes? Did she have Dani's blond hair? Only Aunt Jayne had held her as her heart broke. She'd fled Lincoln and avoided Caleb since. Only Aunt Jayne had brought her back. And now he'd collided into her world. She took a deep breath, then another.

She looked up and caught him watching her. Heat climbed her cheeks and she glanced away. When she looked again, he'd disappeared from the box.

A moment later, a soft knock clicked against the doorframe.

"Ready to talk?" Caleb stood in the doorway, concern filling his eyes.

Dani bristled and glanced at Tricia and Aunt Jayne. "It's about time. I don't know anything that'll help, so let's get started."

He motioned for her to follow him to a bench across the foyer. He cocked his head and slipped a slim notebook from his inside jacket pocket. "Tell me what happened."

Dani told him about the rush to the theater. Finding the box. Trying to talk to the woman in the neighboring box at intermission. Walking into the box when she didn't respond.

"Why did you go in there?'"

Dani closed her eyes, images of how vibrant Renee Thomas had been during the interview filling her mind. "I interviewed her last week. And she seemed so different tonight. She was worried about something. Maybe fearful."

"Why fearful?"

"Last week she couldn't talk enough about her research project.

She vibrated with life. Tonight, well, she looked everywhere but at me. If I remembered her, I know she remembered me. It isn't every day that a grad student gets interviewed."

"Did you notice any changes between your first visit to her box and the second?"

'The air was spicy the second time. Maybe from cologne or aftershave." Dani paused a moment. Even though he might think her suspicious, she had to mention her concern now. "The only other strange thing was the usher."

Caleb looked up from his notes. "An usher?"

"After I discovered the body, a man in a navy blazer kept me corralled next to the box. He insisted I stay in the foyer until you arrived. But others going into the box didn't bother him."

"Do you know his name?"

"No. He didn't tell me and didn't wear a name tag."

"Could you describe him?"

Though she complied readily, Caleb searched her eyes as if she was concealing more about the case. She fought the urge to squirm under the intensity. Her gaze darted to his left hand. It was bare of a ring, not even a shadow of one. "Looks like you're still single."

That ended the scrutiny. "What?"

"Nothing." Dani tightened her lips. How could she have said that? The last thing she wanted to do was relive the past.

"Okay." Caleb dragged the word out. "That's all. Where can I reach you?"

She slipped a card from her purse. "Channel 17. Otherwise, I'm at Aunt Jayne's house." Her cheeks flushed with the memory of their goodnight kisses on the back step.

"Is Logan meeting you here?"

"Huh?" She startled, then stilled. "Yes. Why?"

"Could you take Tricia with you? He can drop her off for me. Otherwise, she'll be stranded here for a long time." "Ever heard of cabs?" Dani bit her lip the moment the words escaped. "That's not what I meant. If she doesn't mind waiting, we can get her home."

"Thanks. Her house is on the way to the station."

Dani shrugged and rolled her eyes. She roused Aunt Jayne from her chair while Caleb told Tricia of the change in plans. In moments she led the others from the box. When she stepped outside, Logan's wave hailed her from a line of trucks.

"Hey, Logan. Hope you brought some coffee."

"Got a cafe mocha just for you. I'm sorry I didn't bring a couple extras." He'd tucked his polo into rumpled khakis, with a Channel 17 baseball cap covering his buzzed hair.

"Aunt Jayne, this is Logan Collins, the best photographer in town. And I take it you already know Tricia."

"Nice to meet you, ma'am. Good to see you again, Tricia." Aunt Jayne tilted her head toward Logan. "Is there somewhere I can sit?"

The area around her aunt's eyes was tightening, a reflection of the confusion that intruded. "Logan, I have to get her home as soon as I can. Can she rest in the Jeep until we're done?" "Sure." They quickly had Aunt Jayne tucked into the front passenger seat with Logan's jacket tucked around her like a blanket. Tricia slipped in behind her and settled in for a chat. Dani heard the murmur of their voices as she focused on the Lied Center.

"Thanks." A smile touched her lips, and she sipped her coffee. "Grab that camera. We've got a lot to do before we call it a night."

Half an hour later, Dani watched people from the medical examiner's office wheel a gurney out the front door of the theater. Hearing footsteps behind her, Dani turned to see Phil Baker, one of Channel 17's evening anchors, walk up. "What are you doing here? The newscast ended a long time ago."

"I was on my way home. Just thought I'd swing by for a minute. See what happened."

Logan crossed his arms and scrutinized Phil. At his closed posture, Dani wondered what Phil had said in those few words to set Logan on edge.

"Well, looks like you kids have it under control. See you tomorrow." He turned on his heel and left them staring at his back. The gathered media followed his progress to his car as if controlled by one puppet master.

"What on earth was that about?" Dani fumed. "Mr. High- and-Mighty thinks we can't handle the story?"

"The theater is not on his way home," Logan said.

3

Investigator Caleb Jamison examined the scene at the plush box for any lingering threads of evidence the crime scene technicians missed. Soon the techs would cart the marked bags of evidence to headquarters for processing.

He sighed in frustration. This murder had the marks of careful premeditation. Few clues were left behind. To have a great shot at clearing the case, he needed a suspect within the first twenty-four hours. With each successive hour, the chance of resolving the case plummeted.

Caleb tucked his chin toward his chest and took a deep breath. Given a case of this visibility, the chief might assign a more experienced investigator in the morning. Any mistakes Caleb made would be blamed on his inexperience.

"I think we're done, Jamison. Here's the lady's purse." Nate Winslow, one of the techs, held out the handbag for him to take. "You can take a quick look before we head to the lab." Caleb put on a pair of gloves. He took the bag and ran his fingers over the outside of the purse before unzipping it. He looked inside and pulled the contents out one by one. "Nothing unusual. Two twenties, a tube of orange lipstick, credit card and ID."

Caleb swept his fingers in the corners of the small handbag. Nothing lay hidden in its inner folds. After returning the contents to the purse, he handed it to the technician.

"Let me know if anything turns up."

"Sure thing. See you back at the station."

He slid his notebook into his inside jacket pocket. *Why would anyone risk killing someone in a very public place like this?* The killer either felt very confident or acted in the passion of a moment.

Whoever killed Ms. Thomas believed he wouldn't be caught.

Dani had noticed he didn't have a ring. Her blush had kept him from admitting he'd noticed the same about her. Her beauty had deepened since that summer when she was sixteen. She wore her hair in a layered cut and looked good. Real good. But she had an edge that hadn't existed then. A feistiness that dared him to get near. Someday he'd tell her how much he regretted the way he'd acted. She'd deserved better, but he'd been so ashamed, he couldn't face her again. In the years since, no one had ever measured up to her.

He shook his head and retrieved his notebook. Time to focus on the task. Interviews indicated that none of the theatergoers who'd contaminated the crime scene had seen or heard anything. The murderer could have been a ghost for all the clues retrieved from the scene. He hoped the crime scene technicians came up with something or the case would be nothing but dead ends.

Heavy footsteps reverberated off the marble floor. Caleb turned to see Officers Jack Denimore and Todd Westmont stride toward him. The two were the Lincoln Police Department's odd couple. Denimore always saw an unsolvable crime, while Westmont's natural optimism was an unusual feature in an investigator. The police had let most of the public leave after the manager announced there would be no second act. Few had volunteered to talk, and they'd retained only those who had entered the box.

"Jamison, I don't think you'll like what we learned." Denimore's haggard expression matched his message. The man looked older than his forty-two years. Caleb's gut tightened.

"He meant he knows you won't like it." Westmont grinned at

Denimore, and then turned to Caleb. "Nobody saw nothing. Nobody heard nothing. The interviews were a bust."

Caleb rubbed his left temple, a vain attempt to slow the pounding that echoed his heartbeat. "Someone saw something. This murder did not happen in a vacuum. More than two thousand people attended the show."

"True, but it happened in a packed theater with everybody focused on the kitty cats onstage. Who's gonna watch the boxes?"

"And if anyone saw anything, they aren't talking." Denimore's scowl deepened, which made his long face appear longer.

Caleb knew Westmont had a point. Most in the audience were honest bystanders who had seen nothing. As much as he hated it that was the reality. Caleb promised himself his first solo case would not become a cold file stuffed in some dank storage room. Each represented a family that waited endlessly for closure. Police might not have found the hit-and-run driver who killed his father, but he'd found a career. The same pain would not linger for this victim's family.

"We know the basic information about her. Chase it down.

Learn who she came to the theater with, and we'll find a witness or her killer." He hoped the trail led somewhere productive.

"And maybe the tooth fairy will put a dollar under my pillow tonight."

"Come on, Denimore. You don't want to lose more of your baby teeth. We'll do this the old-fashioned way and wear out some shoe leather." Westmont looked at Caleb and shrugged his shoulders. "We'll chase down this lady at the station while we wait for forensics."

As the three officers strode out the main doors of the theater, Denimore slowed his long stride at the sight of media vans collected along the edge of the parking lot. Grabbing Caleb by the collar, he hissed, "There's your star witness." Caleb followed Denimore's outstretched arm. Moonlight reflected off Dani's blond hair as she leaned against a Jeep. She looked tired but gorgeous.

Westmont pointed him toward the cameras. "Ready to make a statement?"

With a tight shake of his head, Caleb scanned the assembled reporters, cameras and lights. He saw only piranhas who'd devour him alive. "Nobody tells you talking to the media is part of being an investigator."

"That's why you get paid the big bucks."

Caleb grimaced. It was after ten-thirty, and he'd been up since 6:00 a.m. working another case. Fatigue washed over him. His mind slogged through quicksand as he considered what to say. He rolled his neck in an attempt to loosen the muscles and his growing headache. "Might as well get this over with."

He stepped off the wide veranda and onto the stairs. The reporters shoved a forest of microphones in his face. Trapped, he planted his body.

"Tonight is too early in the investigation to comment. Expect a report on the status sometime tomorrow." After a quick glance at his watch, he locked on Dani. "That's all. Thank you."

Westmont and Denimore stepped in front of him and pushed a path through the small crowd of cameras.

"Come on. Give us something we can use." The assembled media's audible groan followed him down the steps.

"You didn't win any friends in the media with that long- winded speech."

"That's not my job, Denimore. All we know is a young woman named Renee Thomas was killed, probably strangled. We have to notify her relatives before we release details. See you back at the station." Caleb got into his vehicle and sank into the seat. An edge of exhaustion crept over his body and into his mind.

Who was Renee Thomas? If he could answer that question, he'd be able to trace back to who killed her. He doubted she'd attended the theater alone, and Dani seemed to think she'd been waiting for her date. Figure out who'd accompanied Ms. Thomas and he'd have one suspect.

DANI STIFLED a yawn as she watched Logan pack the camera. The night had drained her more than the mini-marathon she'd completed a year earlier. She peeked in the window and noticed Aunt Jayne's mouth open in sleep.

"Ready?" Logan's voice penetrated her scattered thoughts.

"Yeah. Let's get moving, so today can end. Since Andy wants a report for the morning show, I'll head to the station after I get Aunt Jayne home." She scanned the parking lot.

"Your aunt's asleep. Let me give you a ride. Where are you parked?"

Dani rummaged through her handbag for the parking ticket and handed it to him.

"It'll only take a minute to get there. Hop on in."

She pulled herself into the Jeep and tossed her hair over her shoulder. Logan glanced at Tricia in the rearview mirror and smiled. Silence filled the van. Dani watched stores flash by until the parking garage came into view. "Thanks for the lift. Nice to see you again, Tricia."

Logan slid the vehicle into park and waited while she climbed out.

"Be right back." She looked around the outside of the garage for the stairwell on the first floor of the garage. Once she found the right floor, she couldn't miss her bright red Mustang. Arrows pointed to a stairwell across the structure but no signs indicated an elevator. She groaned at the thought of the climb as her feet pinched in the too-tight shoes. Dani scrunched her nose against the odor of trash and too many unwashed bodies. One foot in front of the other, stair after stair. She stopped at the second floor to look for her car, the first words of her package playing in her mind. *Tonight, a murder ruined intermission at the Lied Center for one patron. At this time, police have no suspects.*

Reaching the third-floor stairwell, she walked through the door. Unbidden, her thoughts returned to the body in the box. Had the killer selected the victim at random? Could he have entered her own box and strangled *her* instead? Dani shuddered at the thought. Her breath came in gasps as she sucked in the stale air. The hair on the back of her neck prickled. She scanned the dim floor, looked over her shoulder for the gaze she felt. Nothing. She tried to laugh at her reaction but couldn't find her voice.

"My imagination is running away with me." Shadows shimmied across the empty garage's floors and walls. She quickened her pace.

There. Dani flew to her car. She pulled open her purse. Dug for keys. She yanked them out. Punched the unlock button. She opened the door. Slid behind the wheel.

Inside the locked car, Dani leaned against the steering wheel and inhaled deeply. Closing her eyes, she put the key in the ignition and started the engine. She turned onto the second floor of the garage, and her headlights slid across a man standing by the stairwell door. Her heart skipped. She looked again. Was that the usher from the theater? Involuntarily she stepped on the brake. Watched him drop a cigarette on the pavement and then wipe a handkerchief across his forehead. Looking at her, he stepped on the butt and twisted it into the concrete. His gaze pierced her. Then he started toward her, hands fisted at his sides. She shook herself. Stepped on the gas. His face twisted into an angry scowl. He hit the hood of her car as she drove past.

The tires squealed as she raced around the corner and down the ramp. Why wait for her and then rush her car? Why hit it? Her mind raced to create an explanation.

She reached the exit kiosk and pulled behind Logan. Aunt Jayne eased into the passenger seat of the Mustang. Dani glanced in the rearview mirror but didn't see the usher. Her heart rate calmed, and Dani headed toward Peaceful Estates. Nearly an hour later she pulled into the station parking lot.

She wobbled into the newsroom on the narrow spikes of her sling-back shoes and wished for her more comfortable pumps.

Catcalls laced the air as she headed toward her cubicle. She waved at Mark and Jon, the overnight production assistants.

"Come on, y'all. You should have seen me before I left if you think this looks good."

Dani joined Logan at his editing bay at the back of the cavernous room. She plopped onto a stool and looked at the clock hanging on the wall. It was almost midnight. "Let's get this story together so we can get some sleep before we start all over again."

Logan prepared the deck, and Dani walked into an adjoining sound booth. Her voice sounded as high-pitched to her ear as the first shocking time she'd taped a package. Stepping to the microphone, she ran a sound check. When Logan gave her the thumbs-up, she took a deep breath and voiced the story. This was what she loved about journalism. The pressure to perform. To tell a story without full information. Ad libbing and making it sound polished. Tomorrow the research would kick in, but for now she'd finished her job.

Dani stepped out of the booth and looked at Logan. "Do you want me to pick the video?"

Logan rolled his eyes. "Who's shot video in more countries than you've visited?"

"Well, I've never visited Yemen, but you've got a point. See you in the morning." Dani limped toward the door and her car. "I'll work from home and come in around 11:00 a.m."

She left the building and the image of a well-dressed woman leaning slightly off balance flashed through Dani's mind. A woman who'd wanted to attend *Cats* and return home filled with the music of the show. Instead, her body was en route to the morgue, where a detached stranger would examine it for clues.

Questions raced through her mind. Did the woman know she would die? Had her murderer been a friend, someone she felt safe with? And most important, could Dani have stopped the killer?

4

Silence filled the police station. Caleb stood and stretched. He glanced at his wristwatch and grimaced at the time. It was after three in the morning. Time to move or fall asleep at his desk. While he stared at a wall, a killer roamed.

Yesterday Renee was a twenty-four-year-old graduate student at the university. This morning her corpse rested on a stainless steel gurney in the city morgue. When the registrar's office opened, he'd send Denimore or Westmont down to learn more. Maybe a student or professor had developed an unhealthy interest in her.

She'd lived off campus, apparently by herself. After leaving the theater, he'd driven to her home, and nothing appeared unusual. Technicians were onsite collecting evidence. When they'd finished, he and a couple of officers would examine the house. While there, he'd get a feel for the victim and potential suspects.

Rikki Wilson, the energetic and petite night dispatcher, caught up to him as he headed toward the kitchenette for more coffee. She clucked her tongue. "You look awful. The captain'll arrive in a few hours. Go home and get some sleep."

"I don't have time." It took twenty minutes to drive from the station, time he didn't have.His cabin near Branched Oak was the ideal retreat from homicides on those rare occasions he got time off, and a decent place to live the rest of the time. Unfortunately, tonight was neither of those.

"Then go to your sister's or sleep on the conference room couch. You aren't doing the victim any good tired as you are."

Her motherly advice resonated. If he showed up at this early hour of the morning, he'd scare Tricia to death. So long, soft guest bed. Hello, lumpy conference couch. "Wake me before day shift arrives."

"Sure, honey." The scanner screeched, and Rikki raced to her station.

Caleb pulled a pillow and blanket out of the cluttered closet and studied their rumpled state. When was the last time the pillowcase had seen a washing machine? The aura of dirty gym socks told him not lately. He knew he should care, but his tired body demanded rest over clean sheets. With a sigh, he lowered himself to the couch and shifted until the lumps aligned with his body. He willed his mind to release its questions and welcome sleep.

Thoughts of Dani drifted in. She'd looked real good tonight, but harder around the edges than the girl he remembered. How much of that had he caused? She'd been back in town for months, but he hadn't exactly sought her out. His memories of her were tinged with a shadow of guilt. The kind that came from taking what wasn't his.

He pulled the pillow on top of his head and groaned. Guess he wasn't as free of the past as he'd imagined.

Dani sat in her car in the dark alley behind her home. The small Arts and Crafts home dated to the 1920s. She'd loved visiting when she stayed with Aunt Jayne each summer as a child.

Now an irrational fear pushed her deeper into the seat, and she searched her mind for anyone she could call or stay with. Most of her friends from those long ago summer visits had moved on, and she hadn't bothered to reconnect. Her job took up too much of her schedule to make building friendships easy. Her mind rebelled at the thought of calling Caleb. She could imagine the kind of comfort he'd force on her. That left everyone at work. Just the image she wanted them to have— Dani Richards, reporter extraordinaire, cowering at shadows.

She pushed the car door open and grabbed her briefcase from the passenger seat. She hauled herself from the vehicle, opened the picket fence gate and wobbled up the back porch steps with keys in hand. Tired, she fumbled with the lock.

As she entered the kitchen, peace settled on her. The home retained Aunt Jayne's sweet spirit even though she no longer lived there. Dani kicked off her horrid heels, ready to pitch them in the trash can, and then threw her briefcase onto the island. She crossed the kitchen to the counter for a glass and filled it with water.

The questions and images of the night refused to leave her alone. She leaned against the sink and crossed her arms.

"So much for relaxing at the theater." Who talked to themselves like this? She felt crazy, even though the silence cried for sound. "I need a cat. At least then I'll have someone to talk to." Dani reached around the refrigerator and flipped on the undercounter radio. Strains of classical music filled the air, bringing with it memories of evenings spent dancing with Caleb under the stars. One encounter with him, and he occupied her mind. She shook her head at her foolish heart.

She sipped the water as if it could wash the images away. Aunt Jayne had asked her to stay in the house and pay the utilities and routine upkeep expenses. The house had more room than she could afford on her salary, so she'd gladly accepted. Since she'd arrived, there'd been no time to unpack. That had to change. It was time to admit she was staying. She took her glass of water and headed for her room.

Upstairs, Dani slipped out of her black cocktail dress and into flannel pajamas. She slowly rubbed her feet and the bed with its fluffy pillows and warm comforter beckoned. With a sigh, she returned downstairs. She'd write down everything she'd seen and heard before she allowed herself to sleep. She turned up the soothing music until it filtered from the kitchen into the living room.

Dani slid down the wood floors to the living room. She avoided the prim Victorian couch and opted for the overstuffed chair. She eased into its soft leather, and then tucked her feet underneath her. She grabbed a notepad. Her pen flew as she wrote down every detail including her impressions and guesses. Her mind raced through the events. By the time she finished, Dani felt energized again.

Sleep would be impossible. Since the rest of her books sat in boxes, she wandered over to Aunt Jayne's bookshelves. She slid her fingers along the book spines. Nothing jumped out at her until she saw a Bible tucked on top. Dani couldn't remember the last time she'd voluntarily held a Bible, but Aunt Jayne always valued hers. Maybe the poetry would calm her and help her sleep.

Dani retraced her steps to the chair and opened the book. Its well-worn pages automatically opened to the Book of Psalms. Running her finger down the page, she started to read Psalm 62.

Find rest, O my soul, in God alone; my hope comes from Him. He alone is my rock and my salvation; He is my fortress, I will not be shaken.

The words and the image they conveyed enthralled her. Could He be trusted to be a fortress? After the night she'd lived through, a fortress sounded wonderful.

My salvation and my honor depend on God; He is my mighty rock, my refuge. Trust in Him at all times, O People; pour out your heart to Him, for God is our refuge.

The passage sounded strange yet sweetly familiar. The image of a rock of refuge soothed her, pushing the slide show from the theater from her mind. She clutched the Bible as if it were a lifeline. No matter what she'd seen or the questions chasing her, *He is my mighty rock, my refuge.*

5

H ey, buddy. Wakey, wakey. It's eight-fifteen, and the captain'll catch you sleeping."

Caleb rolled over with a groan. "What time?"

"8:15."

"So much for Rikki waking me up."

"Hey, that's what partners are for." Todd's grin stretched even farther across his face.

"What do you mean 'partners'?"

"Captain's decided I get to babysit you."

"Don't I get a say?" Caleb forced a frown on his face. "Nope. Donaldson's on vacation, Frank got food poisoning last night and Williams is training at the State Patrol Academy. You're stuck with me, buddy boy."

Caleb stretched his arms toward the ceiling as he worked out the kinks. Eyeing Westmont's bright eyes with jealousy, he muttered, "You must have gotten sleep."

"Comfortable sleep. You need a place closer to town. Anything's better than that couch."

"This morning I agree with you, but lakeside living has its advantages."

"I'm waiting to see 'em." Todd hooked his thumbs on his belt loops. "Jack's headed to campus to check with the registrar's office."

"All right. Let's get to work and see if forensics has anything yet."

Westmont studied him a moment before answering. "It's too early for them to process much, but the techs'll finish the house soon. Let's call Ms. Richards and meet her on the way. I want to hear her story myself."

A TRILLING sound echoed from the end of a long tunnel. Its persistent ring tugged Dani from a dream. One filled with the image of a twisted scarf. The trill drilled into Dani's head.

Opening her eyes, she realized she'd slept curled in the oversize chair. She shifted, and a book fell to the floor. Aunt Jayne's Bible. She must have fallen asleep reading it. Despite all that had happened, she'd managed a few hours' sleep. Maybe there was something to the Bible and the God behind it.

As the phone continued to ring, she grabbed the cordless handset from the end table.

"Hello?" Her voice croaked in the stillness.

"Dani Richards, please."

She struggled to place the voice, and cleared her throat. "Yes."

"This is Caleb." At the sound of his tired voice, she tried to sit up despite the blanket tangled around her legs.

"Sounds like you got less sleep than I did."

A sigh echoed across the line. "Probably. I need to ask you a few more questions about last night. Can we get together this morning?"

Nothing on her calendar sounded worse than starting a day with Caleb. To get to the precinct and on to Channel 17 by her eleven o'clock meeting, she'd have to run. "It'll be tough to squeeze in."

"I could meet you somewhere other than the police station."

"My office won't work. Once I'm there, I'm at the mercy of the assignment editor. Maybe I could meet you at the precinct at ten." She looked at the clock and winced. Even if she flew, it wouldn't be possible. "No. Just come to Aunt Jayne's house in forty minutes. I won't have long, but I guess I can answer some questions."

"We'll be there."

Thirty-eight minutes later, a knock sounded. Dani applied the final touches of blush to her cheeks with shaking hands. The thought of Caleb in her house caused her stomach to lurch and made her feet want to bolt. She hesitated as long as possible before opening the door. Caleb looked weighed down, with bags under his eyes. The man next to him had copper hair and a grin that prompted her to smile in response.

"Good morning. Come in." She stepped back to allow them to enter.

Caleb pushed from the doorpost and walked in. "This is my partner, Officer Todd Westmont. You probably saw him last night."

Dani shook her head. "No. It's nice to meet you, Officer Westmont. Would either of you like coffee? I have a fresh pot."

Caleb nodded. "Sounds great. Black's fine."

She led them to the kitchen. "Have a seat at the island. Anything for you, Officer?"

"No, thanks."

She poured two cups and handed one to Caleb. "How can I help?" She pulled a stool around the island and took a seat.

"We wanted to review a couple things with you." Caleb pulled a notebook from his jacket pocket. It looked like the same jacket he'd worn the previous night. "You knew the victim?" "Not really. I interviewed her about a week ago for a report on food safety. It was hard to understand the topic, but she loved her research."

Officer Westmont leaned his large frame on the island. "Mind telling me what you saw?"

"I entered her box when Aunt Jayne wandered in before the show. At intermission I remembered who she was, and looked in to say 'Hi.' It wasn't until I faced her that I realized she was dead."

The officers reviewed the details with her, but she couldn't add anything to what she'd told Caleb the previous night. "I wish I had more to tell you, but I didn't see or hear anything." Dani paused and poured more cream into her coffee. As she watched the coffee and cream swirl together, she searched her thoughts. "She must have struggled, but I was focused on the stage. *Cats* isn't exactly a quiet musical."

She lifted her chin and met Officer Westmont's questioning gaze. "After I talked to you, I think I saw the usher in the parking garage. A man waited on the second floor and tried to stop the car." Dani searched for the right words to describe his behavior. "I felt like someone watched me on the second floor, and he seemed so angry. And almost frantic. I don't know why." Caleb considered her, and she fought the warming sensation that spread across her. "We'll try to find him. It would help if you could tell us anything else about him."

Dani lifted her chin. "Sorry, he didn't volunteer his name, and I was focused on the dead body."

"We don't have much to go on."

"Fine. I'll find him."

"That isn't your job. Leave that to the police."

Dani gritted her teeth. Caleb wasn't the only one with investigative skills. She vowed to find out more about the usher before the police did.

He rolled his eyes. "I see you're still stubborn. Who did you talk to about the murder?"

"Andy Garrison, a producer at the station, and Logan Collins, the photographer with me." Dani looked at her watch, ready to end the conversation. "I have to leave now to get to work."

Both men pushed back from the island and stood. Caleb reached into a pocket and pulled out a card. He handed it to her. "My cell's on the back. Call if you remember anything."

Ten minutes after their departure, Dani pulled into the station parking lot and scrambled out of her car. With a quick hello to the receptionist, she raced through the lobby and into the newsroom.

The studio and advertising offices dominated the station, leaving a large room filled with cubicles for the news team. Dani entered the cavern and absorbed the chaos as the familiar insanity calmed her.

The assignment editor sat at the front surrounded by whiteboards showing three days' worth of assignments. As she walked to her cubicle, the day assignment editor's shout followed her. "I need to talk about your assignment."

Vic Davis juggled the phone and scanners like a pro, but Dani never found herself on his good side.

"Kate wants you on the theater-killing story." He grunted out the words.

She flashed her best Katie Couric smile at him. "That's why I'm here."

His dour expression deflected her smile. "Play things up with the police." With that, Vic returned to his kingdom and its telephone chime.

They needed to get rolling on the story. Dani glanced around the newsroom for Logan. Kate Johannson, the tiny news director with a nose for what viewers wanted, waved Dani to her office.

Logan reclined on the love seat in the office. "You're slow this morning."

"I'm here now. I've already talked to the police this morning."

Kate settled in behind her desk. "Today you're slated for live shots on the 5:30 and 10:00 p.m. shows, as well as shorter packages during the other newscasts. The noon show is covered. I want you to figure out who the victim is so we can tell her story today."

"We already know her name. I interviewed her last week. Haven't the police released her identity?" Dani looked from Logan to Kate, brow wrinkled.

"They haven't said anything." Kate crossed her arms, and let silence linger.

"Kate, her name is...Renee Thomas, though I need to verify it."

"Do it and get the name in a story. Don't stand there like a decoration."

Dani pirouetted on her pointed heel and left Kate's office. Logan stood at an edit bay, arms crossed. She quickened her pace, oblivious to the clatter of noise in the background.

"Ready to get to work?"

"You can't release the name, Dani."

Dani opened her mouth to argue back. "Why? Trying to do my job, too? Who do you think you are?" With each syllable her voice rose. She was moments from losing control in front of her colleagues. She spun away from Logan. "Outside...now." Reaching the exit, she pounded on the release bar. With a satisfying thud the lock released and the door flew open. Blinking in the bright sunlight, she stepped past the doorway. A shadow grazed her when Logan joined her in the parking lot.

"Logan, you are the best photographer I've worked with, but you are not a reporter. That's my job."

Logan stepped out of the doorway. "You've known Caleb as long as I have. You're making a mistake if you release the victim's name before he releases the information."

"He never asked me to hold it back. It won't hurt anybody unless she has a secret life." Nervous energy propelled Dani back and forth in the parking lot. "This is my story. I found the body, and I knew Renee. I owe it to her and the station to get this right. This is our break. We have a window when we know something no one else does. We'll make the most of it." His brows knit together, and he remained silent.

"Unless you give me a good reason. I'm running with it. If you won't help, I'll get a photographer who will." Dani winced. The words sounded more threatening than she'd intended. Logan nodded. "All right. Let's get to work."

"Grab your equipment and meet me at my desk."

Logan returned to the editing bays on the inside wall of the newsroom as Dani charged to her cubicle. Half of the cubes were empty. With five shows scattered across the day, the reporters and anchors rarely overlapped. That happened on exceptional days like 9/11 or the launch of a war.

Dani grabbed a notepad from the pile that teetered on the edge of her desk. Logan pulled a chair around and straddled it. Before Dani could open her mouth, Kate approached.

"Glad to see you two made up. Dani, track down everything you can about the victim. We need more than her name by five-thirty. I want her to come alive. Logan, have your buddy at the police station confirm her name. Isn't he in charge of this investigation?" As Logan nodded, Kate glanced at her Rolex. "We've got fifteen minutes to airtime. Dani, you'll do an onset report."

Adrenaline surged through Dani at the new deadline as she watched Kate storm back to her office. "There went my five hours to prepare. Is she always this intense?"

"Only when the story's big, and we have an edge. I'll call Caleb."

"Wait." Dani turned to her open notepad. The victim's name wasn't enough to fill a report in fifteen minutes. And she couldn't release the name without confirmation. "Can you find the tape of our interview with Renee? From last week?"

Logan nodded. "I'm on it."

He sprinted toward the tape room. Dani crossed her fingers. This had to work or her silence was all that'd fill the air during the newscast.

She quickly outlined talking points and uploaded them on the network. The producer would call them up for Dani to ad lib from when Rochelle tossed the newscast to her.

That taken care of, Dani typed Renee Thomas and Lincoln into a search engine. Five hundred results. She hoped a handful highlighted *her* Renee Thomas but would settle for one.

Glancing at her watch, she put her computer in hibernate mode, grabbed her jacket and hustled to the studio for the noon newscast. She hurried to the mounted mirror and counter inside the door to touch up her makeup. Unlike her time in St. Louis, here she had to apply her own. She topped it all off with a coat of powder and walked to the side where the director could signal her to join the anchors.

She resisted the urge to rock on her heels as she waited. Each sound echoed off the studio's concrete floor, and the sensitive microphones the anchors wore picked up everything. Would Logan find the interview tape? The floor director flashed a hand signal. She had thirty seconds to get seated and micced. She slid an earpiece on and heard Tori talking to an assistant producer.

Dani cut in. "Tori, did Logan get you the tape?"

"Not yet. He's trying to cue it up."

"I need it now."

"Do what you're paid to do. Ad lib."

Dani painted a smile on her face and faced a camera as the package wrapped up. Without the video confirmation she had nothing to report. Logan entered the studio. She quirked an eyebrow at him, and he shook his head.

Rochelle Nicholson raised a perfectly waxed eyebrow and looked at Dani. "Dani Richards joins us on set with the latest on last night's murder at the Lied Center. Dani."

Dani smiled at Rochelle. Taking a deep breath, she turned to camera two. She imagined Aunt Jayne on the other side of the lens. "Last night, a university graduate student was murdered during act 1 of *Cats.*" She filled in the few details that she could, before turning back to the anchor. "Rochelle, police ask that anyone having any information about this crime call the Crime Watchers' hotline."

"Thanks, Dani. When we return, Mike will fill us in on the weekend weather."

A commercial filled the air, and Dani slipped off the microphone. She left the studio and ran headlong into Kate Johannson.

"Miss Richards. Please come to my office for a moment." Underneath her calm demeanor, a bright red climbed Kate's neck.

Dani braced herself for a torrent of words. Kate liked to pull staff into her office and berate them.

"I expected more in your report. Didn't you forget something?"

"No. I reported everything I could without outside confirmation. We raced to confirm the victim's name but couldn't. Logan and I will find that tape."

"The police haven't denied her name, right?"

Dani nodded.

"You blew an opportunity—one delivered on a platter. Get your confirmation, or *I'll* run her name and this will no longer be your story."

6

Caleb pulled up to the victim's house and parked behind the crime scene van. His contacts scratched his dry eyes, but his glasses sat at his cabin. He and Dani had spent a summer racing around the lake on his Jet Ski. The innocent sparkle and joy that had filled her eyes had disappeared. How much of that came from her job that forced her to see too much darkness? That aspect paralleled his career. Could they build something from the ruins of the past? He wanted the answer to be yes, but ten years ago Dani refused to see him after the night he'd pushed things too far. Based on her reaction during the last twenty-four hours that hadn't changed.

The deep rattle of a vehicle that could only be Westmont's caught his attention and pulled him from the past. The engine quieted down with a last hiccup.

"Sounds even worse than last week." Caleb walked toward the car with a grin. He tapped the hood and watched Westmont leap from the car.

"Careful." Westmont's expression flashed pain. "The mechanics only made her worse."

"That's possible?"

A screen door slammed, and Caleb looked up to see the techs exit the house. Now he could walk through the rooms, and if lucky, learn something about Renee Thomas's killer.

Caleb deposited his empty cup inside his car and started up the sidewalk. Westmont caught up as they flashed their badges to the officer posted at the door.

Renee's bungalow was built in the 1930s. The tiny porch contained a single plastic chair which one stiff Nebraska wind would blow across the yard like a tumbleweed. From the front door, Caleb could see through to the back door. No photos or prints hung on the bland beige walls. She'd expended no effort to make the house a home. Either she rented or lacked the interest to decorate.

The office filled with bookshelves, file cabinets and an over-flowing desk beckoned him from the right of the entry way. A bonanza of personal information waited. "I'll start here."

"Glad to leave you the paper. Can't stand the paper cuts. I'll check her bedroom." Westmont disappeared down the hallway.

Caleb pulled on a pair of gloves and opened drawers and rifled papers. The drawers contained a haphazard assortment of bills and advertisements shoved on top of pens, notepads and stamps. How had she located anything in that jumble?

He pulled open the file cabinet. Cleanly labeled folders lined the first drawer in contrast to the messy desk. Satellite. Phone. Credit Cards. He pulled those files out.

Next, he grabbed a file labeled House and opened it.

The file contained a copy of the recorded deed, purchase agreement and her real estate taxes. He didn't know many graduate students who owned houses, even small ones. Maybe a wealthy uncle or grandpa had helped her.

The doorbell rang. The officer standing guard should intercept the visitor. When the doorbell rang again, Caleb craned his neck to see who stood on the porch. The angle was all wrong and none of the vehicles on the street looked familiar.

The doorbell rang a third time, and Westmont strode down the hallway.

Caleb waved him into position behind the door. "Coming." "Five bucks says media's on the other side."

Caleb raised his eye to the peephole. With a flourish he opened the door. "Dani Richards."

"Hello, Caleb." She smiled up at him with a lovely sparkle in her eyes and stepped closer. "I wondered if I could look around since the crime scene guys are gone. Hmm. She didn't decorate much."

Caleb stifled a grin at the cute way she tried to slip past him. He had to hand it to her. The woman had gumption. "You know I can't do that, Dani."

"I found the victim. Doesn't that earn me one look?" She flashed a flirtatious smile that he soaked in for a moment. She must really want to see what was inside to try to blind him with the charm that had been absent the day before.

"I wish I could, but I'd violate all kinds of procedure. Can't let you disturb evidence."

"I only want to look around. I didn't even bring a camera." "Nope. Can't do it. I'd be happy to walk you to your car though." Caleb eased out the door and closed it behind him.

Dani's smile turned into an expression that could freeze a lake in an instant. "You won't help."

"Not today."

"Thanks a lot." Her eyes sparked at him as she spit the words out. "Don't bother walking me to my car."

Caleb watched until Dani's car pulled onto the street. He shook his head at her antics. Dani reminded him a lot of his sister, and he couldn't give that compliment to many women. Too bad she'd hate him for the rest of her life. Where had the officer gone? If disappearing on the job was a regular practice, he'd stay a junior officer for the rest of his career.

"Westmont, any idea where our guard went?"

"Nope. I'll check out back. I bet he's stretching his legs."

"Thanks." Caleb returned to the House file. He scanned the deed and stopped cold. He reread the document. Phil Baker. Evening anchor at Channel 17. Dani Richards's station. Did she know the connection?

He set the deed aside for Westmont.

The purchase agreement came next. Caleb's jaw dropped when he saw the price. Renee brought the house from Phil Baker two months earlier for twenty-five thousand dollars. He wasn't a real estate agent, but the house could sell for a hundred and twenty-five thousand more. Caleb jotted down questions he wanted to ask Mr. Baker, like why he sold the house for a song.

Binders labeled Research stood on their sides in the bottom drawer. The well organized volumes looked to contain notes about her university projects. He'd assign those beasts to someone else.

He closed the file drawer. Bookshelves sagged under the weight of textbooks, an eclectic mix of science and psychology. She'd won a fellowship to the University of Nebraska. Maybe the fellowship had conditions attached to it.

The floor squeaked, and Caleb turned from the bookshelves.

"Johnson's back out front." Westmont pulled a small porcelain picture frame from his jacket pocket. "Recognize this guy?"

Caleb took the frame and examined the picture. Renee at a football game with her arm wrapped around a man most in the city recognized. "Phil Baker. Ties into what I wanted to show you. He sold Miss Thomas this house far under market value two months ago." Caleb flipped the folder to Westmont.

"I can't tell for sure from the photo, but it looks like they were good friends. If he sold this house on the cheap, it makes me think they were more."

"I agree. We'll question him about this. What else did you find?"

"Only what I expect to see in a lady's bathroom and bedroom. She lived alone. I didn't see doubles of anything to suggest a frequent guest."

Caleb looked around the office while he considered their next step. "I've searched the files. Did anything clue you into who she went to the theater with last night? Maybe a letter with her ticket?"

"Nada. She has a paperless bedroom. Not even a book on the

bedside table." Westmont nodded at the sagging bookshelves. "She kept 'em all here."

"Let's search the living room and kitchen before we head back. Maybe we'll find something—information about a car, or a calendar."

Caleb walked through the kitchen. It was as bare of personal details as the other rooms. A tiny table perched against a wall with two folding chairs tucked under it. The small window above the sink had no curtains. Opening the refrigerator door, he saw an impressive collection of condiments but little else. He didn't know if a woman could live on ketchup and dressing alone, but she'd tried.

Turning his back on the kitchen, he wandered into the living room. *Who were you, Renee Thomas? And why is your house so empty of personality ?*

Caleb watched Westmont remove each cushion from the couch to examine underneath them. "Find anything?"

"Nope, just a few quarters." Westmont flipped the final cushion in place.

Caleb grabbed a couple boxes from the office doorway. "Let's head back."

When he reached the station, he went straight to the conference room with the boxes.

Had the chaplain's office contacted Renee's family yet? If so, the chief could release her name. If not, they'd wait. The worst experience of his life had occurred when he learned from an impersonal television that his father had died. He wanted to spare her family that.

Caleb had commandeered the conference room for the investigation. Fortunately, Lincoln had little violent crime, so the extra space was his until the case cleared.

"Jamison, you'd better get over here."

"What?" Caleb stuck his head above the dividers and searched for the voice.

"Over here. I'm in the break room. You'll want to see this." Caleb recognized Officer Chapman's voice.

As Caleb walked into the break room, his eyes glanced at the television sitting in the corner. A banner marched across the bottom of its twenty-seven-inch screen. "Renee Thomas, identified as woman murdered at Lied Center. More at five."

He closed his eyes. Opened them to the same words. His jaw clenched. Who released her name? Dani?

7

D ani fumed at the appearance of a police car behind her as she raced to campus. She eased off the gas. A delay and ticket were the last things she needed. She'd wasted time driving to the Thomas home only to blow her opportunity.

Her calls had turned up a Dr. Bartholomew to interview. He'd told her he'd be happy to discuss Renee Thomas and would be in his office all afternoon. Now if she could only find Findley Hall and some parking. Dani caught sight of the ten story building and pulled into a space out front.

"All right, Dr. Bartholomew. Where are you hiding?" Climbing nine flights of stairs wasn't her idea of fun. Dr. Bartholomew's office was on the eighth floor. The elevator doors opened and she stepped inside.

After circling the floor twice, she found the office tucked in a corner.

The door stood open, so she rapped on the doorframe. Rows of bookshelves lined the wall opposite the door as she waited for the call to enter. After a minute she rapped louder.

"Stop knocking and come in." The gruff voice sounded impatient.

"Hello, sir. I'm Dani Richards with Channel 17. We spoke earlier."

"Yes, yes. Have a seat." The seventy-something professor examined her over his tortoiseshell glasses. "So how can I help?" "How did you know Renee Thomas?"

"You mean that poor girl killed last night? No, she wasn't here long. I wouldn't have her as a student until her dissertation." "Do you know anything about her research?"

"The department buzzed with the possibilities. That young woman was close to creating a process that would make it virtually impossible to insert harmful agents into the food supply. Since 9/11, it's been a hot research area. And her fellowship focused on that area."

"Which fellowship?"

"She was a Cornelius fellow. There are two a year, and Mr. Cornelius likes to pit the recipients against each other to solve a manufacturing or product development problem his company has." Dr. Bartholomew tented his fingers together on top of his desk. "This year he asked his fellows to tackle a safety issue. Ms. Thomas made a breakthrough that could change the way companies formulate their products. I wonder how her fellowship contract was drafted."

"I'm not sure I follow. Why would that be important?" "Because most contracts call for all research and new products and processes developed here at the university to be patented by the researcher and assigned or loaned to the university. Occasionally, the company who funds the research keeps the rights to the results, but that's rare. A misunderstanding could arise if a company was unused to the university's system of funded research and realized too late it couldn't profit."

"How long has Mr. Cornelius funded these fellowships?" "Approximately two years."

"So you're telling me a company could provide funding to the university for a specific area of research and never receive anything in return?"

"Nothing monetary. The company benefits from the results of the research but won't get the patent and the wider monetary gain from holding that patent. They'll also receive a tax deduction."

"Would Ms. Thomas work on her own? Or would she be part of a team with a professor and other grad students?"

"It varies. Cornelius fellows work under Professor Marcy Irvine, but you'll have to check with her on the structure of Miss Thomas's fellowship. She's on sabbatical in Zaire until August. The department staff could tell you how to contact her." Dr. Bartholomew glanced at his watch. "I've enjoyed our time, but I must run. Call if I can provide additional assistance." "Thanks for your time, Professor." After they shook hands, Dani ducked into a small library at the end of the hallway. She'd grasped half of what Bartholomew said and wanted to organize her thoughts on paper before she forgot the key details. Would someone kill over academic research?

The question nagged at her as she returned to the station. As the bell from the church across the street bonged four times, Dani entered. Logan waved her across and pointed toward the control room. "Tori released the victim's name." Dani burst through the door into the control room. The heavily air-conditioned space produced instant goose bumps on her arms that even her rage couldn't reduce.

Tori sat at her producer desk, pounding on her keyboard. "It's about time you got back."

Renee's name ran across the bottom of the television. "How could you release the name without clearing it with me?" "Last time I checked, you aren't the news director. You've known the name for hours and didn't do anything. Now it's out. Lucky for you we beat the competition." Tori sat back in her chair, disdain dripping from her.

Dani wanted to scrub the smug look from Tori's face. "There is such a thing as confirming a source. That's journalism 101." Dani struggled to keep sarcasm from coloring her tone. "And what if her family hasn't been notified yet? They don't need to learn something like that via TV."

"Unlike you, I got confirmation. Here's your fax with a copy of the victim's driver's license."

She snatched the page from Tori's grasp with shaking fingers. The face that haunted her smiled from the picture. "That wasn't the way to reveal the name."

"Take your confirmation and get a package together for the five-thirty newscast." With a toss of her sleek ponytail, Tori swiveled her chair and left Dani staring at her back.

Clutching the fax, Dani smoothed out the crumpled edges and went to search for Logan. One biting sentence from Tori scorched everything around her. She had thirty minutes to create a package. Glancing at the clock that dominated the front wall of the control room, adrenaline spiked her system.

"Renee Thomas, University of Nebraska graduate student, murdered at theater." Caleb read the scrolling words as shock colored his mind.

"We haven't released that information." The words whistled between clenched teeth.

The buttery smell of popcorn filled the small break room and turned Caleb's stomach. He headed toward the nearest desk and phone as the words continued across the bottom of the screen.

"Somebody get me the number for Channel 17. I want to know why that station released my victim's name. And I want to know now."

Officer Chapman jumped from his seat and scrambled to find a phone book. Other officers wandered past the desk, slowing their steps until Caleb threw a hard look.

"Hey, you look ready to explode, and it's not your best look." At Westmont's voice, Caleb looked up from drumming his fingers against the desk. He'd throttle someone when he figured out who'd leaked the name. Westmont ambled through the station from the vehicle entrance with an empty box swinging at his side.

"I've got it." Chapman yelled the number to him. Caleb scratched the number into his notebook.

Caleb dialed the number, and Westmont grabbed his shoulder. "What's going on? Angry is not a good way to call the media." Caleb shook Westmont's arm off and turned back to the phone. "It's the perfect mood to be in when a TV station released the name of our victim. We can't surprise Baker now." "That's it? That's why you're upset?" Westmont grinned at him. Westmont took the phone from Caleb and returned it to its portal. "You've gotta lighten up, or this job'll kill you." Caleb pulled in a deep breath. He couldn't let his frustration with dead ends color his work. Other than interviewing Phil Baker, he didn't have a whole lot to go on. The chief's deadline for answers would require Caleb to put in another long night tracking down nonexistent leads. "Let's interview Phil Baker and figure out his involvement."

"Something feels off about that one. Do you want to make it easy for him, let him come in between shows or tomorrow morning?" Westmont reviewed his notes. "Or bring him in now?"

Caleb shook his head. "We don't have enough for a warrant yet, so let's keep this friendly. We might avoid a lawyer that way."

8

A murmur swept through the newsroom. Dani glanced up from her cube. The newscast had been flawless, and Tori had even looked relaxed when she stepped out of the control room, unlike her rattled demeanor when the rundown exploded during the 5:30 newscast.

Caleb and that other officer strode through the newsroom. Three months in town without seeing him and now she couldn't avoid him. Dani eased out of her chair to get a better look.

"Looks like they're headed to the conference room." Logan joined her. "Glad we found that tape in time."

"Renee was so excited during it. I almost hoped we had the wrong person."

Caleb breezed past her.

Dani gritted her teeth and turned her back. Caleb could do whatever he wanted, she needed to work. At five-thirty, she'd told viewers Ms. Thomas was a well liked grad student at the university, and had shown a clip from the interview. Somehow, by this time tomorrow, Dani would find a way to make Renee Thomas more than a statistic.

After thinking through her options, Dani stood and headed toward the assignment desk.

"LeAnn, who's available to shoot in the morning?" "You'll need someone on a Saturday?" LeAnn Roberts, the weekend assignment editor, sounded dubious.

"I'll keep working the theater murder. There's a meeting of ushers at the Lied I need to attend. Not much more I can learn here behind a desk."

"Have you talked to Kate or Tori about this?"

"Kate told me to run with the story."

LeAnn swiveled her chair and scrutinized the whiteboard behind her desk as she twisted her fingers in her dark curls. "Logan's free early in the morning, but you'll have to leave by nine. Otherwise, you're stuck with the new kid, and you don't want that."

Dani grimaced at the thought. Vinnie Carloni had been with the station three weeks and still didn't know the equipment. His shots were useless.

"Thanks. I'll make sure I'm here." Dani headed back toward her cube. Ready to wait Caleb out. She needed to know who he talked to and why. Even if the thought of asking him for anything caused her head to pound.

CALEB REVIEWED his notes while he and Todd waited in the station's conference room. It wasn't large, only ten by twelve feet, but big enough to talk with Mr. Baker. At the sound of the door, he turned his attention from the plaques on the wall. He knew Baker instantly. His square jaw and rugged looks made him easy on the camera. Baker eased into the chair closest to the door the moment he walked into the room.

A petite, middle-aged woman accompanied Baker. Energy radiated from her in stark contrast to Baker's deliberate control. "You must be Investigator Jamison and Officer Westmont. I'm Kate Johannson, the news director." She stretched a hand across the table.

Her bluntness pushed Caleb back in his chair for a minute. The woman wanted to control the situation. He took the proffered hand.

"I'm Investigator Jamison. Officer Westmont and I have a few questions for Mr. Baker. You'll need to leave."

She smiled as she tilted her chin to meet his gaze. "I'll be happy to leave in a moment. While I'm a journalist first, I'm also Mr. Baker's employer. As his employer, I must know whether you intend to arrest him."

"Actually, ma'am, you don't. This is an ongoing police investigation, and unless you're his attorney or want to tell me something you know about Mr. Baker and his relationships with women, you'll have to leave."

"Point taken. Phil, should I call anyone for you?"

Phil looked up from the table with steadiness. "Nope. This won't take long."

"All right. I'll leave you to your conversation."

Caleb watched her walk out of the room with a regal bearing. Turning back to the table, he took a seat and leaned toward Baker. "We have a few questions for you. You have the right to an attorney. Anything you say can be used against you in a court of law."

"I don't have anything to hide."

"Then let's get started. How long have you known Renee Thomas?"

The silence thickened until the tick of the second hand on the clock echoed. Baker directed his gaze to Caleb. "What do you think I have to do with her?"

Caleb narrowed the space between them as he leaned across the table. "We know you sold her a house under market value. I want to understand why. Out of the kindness of your heart?"

"The house needed work. I put it on the market a year ago. Nobody gave it a glance until she came around. When she wanted it, I jumped."

Baker's answer almost made sense, but the Cheshire cat grin he flashed at the end hit Caleb the wrong way. He leaned back in his chair and studied Baker.

"Why would she want a home improvement project? I didn't see tools around the house, and it was in decent shape. Busy grad students don't take on renovation projects."

"I don't know what she did. You'll have to ask someone who knew her." Phil cleared his throat. As he spoke, he looked each man in the eye. "I don't know why she liked the house. Maybe the thought of buying it from someone all her friends would recognize appealed to her."

"I'm sure that happens all the time. Strangers want to buy things from you just because you're on TV." Caleb didn't try to keep the sarcasm from his words.

Todd pushed off the wall where he'd stood during the interchange and settled into a chair. Baker shuffled in his seat as Todd crowded his space.

Caleb eased back at the signal. Time to get comfortable and let Mr. Good Cop enter the conversation.

"I need to ask you a question about something we found at the house. You said you met Ms. Thomas at closing."

"I didn't go to closing. My realtor handled it for me." Phil fidgeted with his cufflinks. His fingers focused on the right one, then switched to the left. Back and forth in a nervous twitch.

"Then can you tell me who is in this picture with Ms. Thomas?" Todd pulled out the snapshot from Renee's bedroom. Caleb scrutinized Baker as he took the photo.

Phil paled under his makeup. With effort he dragged his eyes from the photo to each officer and back to the photo. "Where did you find this?"

"In her bedroom. Stuck in a corner of a mirror. She must have enjoyed looking at it." Todd scooted back from the table.

"I didn't remember until you showed me this. I might have met her at a friend's tailgate. People hound me for pictures. I can't remember every person."

No matter what question he asked, Caleb couldn't get Phil to budge from that answer. Ten minutes later, they left Phil in the conference room. The guy would need a new shirt. For someone who didn't have anything to hide, he'd acted more than a little worried.

Caleb's stomach insisted it was time to eat, so he grabbed take-out on the way to the police station. Caleb walked into the conference room bearing steaming bags of Chinese food.

Denimore looked up. "Hope you brought me some moo goo gai pan." He shook his head and grimaced. "This research is indecipherable. I understand every other page."

"Do what you can with it. Baker was less than honest with us, so Todd and I'll work that angle until we know why he lied." Todd walked to the table and rifled through the box. "Don't touch my research," Denimore growled. "It's enough of a mess without you disturbing it."

Shaking his hand in mock pain, Todd grinned. "Fine. Don't be too quick to zero in on Baker, Caleb. The fact Baker's not honest doesn't mean he killed Renee Thomas. We'll see who purchased the theater tickets." Todd headed toward the front desk. Five minutes later he returned with empty hands.

"We don't know anything other than the person who bought the tickets paid cash. I'll take pictures of Baker and a few others by tomorrow, but looks like we won't get an easy answer."

"So nothing's being handed to us. Let's focus on motive. Why kill Ms. Thomas?"

WHEN SHE GOT HOME, Dani prepared a mug of hot chocolate and sat at the dining room table. Aunt Jayne had calligraphed verses two feet from the top of the barn red wall. She turned in the chair as she read the gold letters circling the ceiling. *Find rest, O my soul, in God alone; my hope comes from Him. He alone is my rock and my salvation.* No wonder the words had whispered familiar comfort to her heart last night.

Dani pondered the meaning, but the words remained cloaked combinations of letters. She finished the cup and then headed upstairs for bed.

The shrill tone of the phone pierced the darkness. She groped for it on the bedside table, heart racing. "Hello?"

"I'm watching." Static cackled in her ear.

"Who is this?"

"End your investigation now."

"What are you talking about?"

Maniacal laughter filled her ear. Dani dropped the phone. Shudders coursed through her as echoes of the laugh ricocheted around the room. She hung up the phone and sat up. hugging her knees. Her mind raced over the call. She didn't know who the caller was, and it certainly wasn't the first such call in her career, though certainly the strangest. One call would not scare her away from an investigation. If anything, it made her more determined to find Renee's killer.

The next morning, she met Logan at the station for their interviews.

"You wouldn't believe the call I got last night."

"Anything to worry about?"

"Just someone telling me they're watching." Dani shrugged. "Takes more to scare me off a story. The police are focused on Phil as the murderer, but he has too much to lose." "Unless he killed her to prevent their relationship going public."

"You're assuming they had one. Maybe they had something going, but Renee talked to someone. We need to find that person. We'll start on campus, but if we can't find someone there we'll talk to her neighbors. I want to see who else was in her life." Dani watched the houses turn to stores around Twenty-seventh Street, before becoming apartment buildings that melted to the outskirts of campus.

"It's a long shot on a Saturday." Logan turned left onto Sixteenth Street and a parking lot near the student union.

"Maybe, but we also have a meeting at the Lied Center at lunch. We'll find something." Dani opened her door and took in the stately brick buildings and open acres of lawn set in a loose courtyard. Logan popped the back of the Jeep and pulled out his equipment. "Let's start around Findley Hall."

Dani pulled a thin bag out of her briefcase before tucking the case between the seats. Throwing the strap over her shoulder, Dani followed the sidewalk to Findley Hall's stone facade. "Looks like the money ran out when they built this hall." "Actually it's native limestone, so quite Nebraskan."

Dani rolled her eyes at Logan's explanation. "What is it about Nebraska that makes residents so proud of all things Nebraskan?" She scanned the area, but it was empty of students or any traffic. She turned around, looking for someone to approach. "Okay. Administrative buildings are closed because it's Saturday. No students are hanging out right now. Let's see what we can find inside."

They climbed the stairs and walked through the heavy door. Every room on the first floor was locked, and the building looked as empty as the sidewalks.

"What now, boss?"

"Renee's grad student office was up on the eighth floor. Let's get b-roll of that and the building. Then we'll go to the usher meeting." Dani tried to ignore the vague feeling of disappointment that pushed against her. She'd known it was a long shot, but really hoped she'd find someone here, even if it was a Saturday. Logan shot enough background shots to fill a dozen packages. "Come on, we've got to hike over to the Lied."

Maybe, just maybe, she'd get lucky and the usher she was searching for would attend.

9

T he Lied Center's stone facade towered over Dani. Sunlight gleamed off the windows that covered the front, and she looked away. A matinee of *Cats* was scheduled, so the box office had opened at eleven o'clock. "We're supposed to enter through the box office doors," Dani told Logan.

"You're wearing your game face," he said.

"I'm ready for a few answers."

Logan backed through the box office doors and held them for Dani. She followed the hallway that ran alongside the office. Her heels sunk into the plush carpet and the lingering scent of hundreds of perfumes tickled her nose.

"The lady on the phone said most ushers should attend the meeting," Dani said. "Why don't you set up in the hallway while I look for him."

"The lighting looks good here. I'll stick my head in once I'm ready."

Dani entered the large conference room. About fifty people sat in clusters around tables arranged in a large square. Attendees ate while a woman dressed in a tailored peach suit reviewed policies posted on the front wall. A man handed Dani a stapled copy of the policies that contained a plan for future emergencies. She tucked the paper into her bag, then examined each face. None matched the usher she wanted.

When Logan appeared in the doorway, she shook her head. *He's not here,* she mouthed.

"Are there any questions?" Sleepy looks greeted the moderator's question. "That's all I have. Thank you."

Dani pushed away from the wall and approached the woman. "Hi, I'm Dani Richards. I believe we spoke yesterday."

"Susan Thompson."

"The usher I came to see isn't here. Could you help me figure out who he is?"

"I can try, but understand we have over a hundred fifty volunteer ushers, fifty of whom work any given show. I interact with each one no more than a handful of times."

"Is there someone who coordinates volunteers for specific performances?"

"Yes. Lisa sat in on the meeting." Susan glanced at her watch and then back at Dani. "The man you described doesn't ring a bell. We should have a sign-in list though. I'll find Lisa and send her here with the sheet."

"This usher worked on the upper floor near the boxes. He stopped me from leaving after the murder."

Dani followed Susan out of the conference room and stopped short when she caught Logan interviewing a volunteer. She waited until the person had stepped away and then approached Logan. "Learn anything?"

"A couple worked Thursday night but didn't see anything. I got their reactions and asked if they'd volunteer again."

"Let me guess. They will."

"Of course." Logan put a pious expression on his face.

"The arts are an important part of our community. Ready for me to pack up?"

"Wait a minute." Dani spotted Susan and another woman headed toward her. "I hope that's Lisa and she has information we can use."

She hurried to meet the women while Logan leaned against the wall near his gear.

Susan introduced Dani. "I'll leave you two to talk."

Dani liked Lisa from the moment they shook hands. Her smile radiated warmth tinged with concern. Dani described the usher to her and waited for any sign Lisa recognized him.

Lisa looked at a piece of paper she held in her hand. "That usher could be Michael Stevens. He's volunteered for a couple Broadway shows. Volunteers love those performances."

"Do you have contact information for him?"

"I'm not free to share it with you. We guard the confidentiality of our volunteers."

For someone who valued privacy, Lisa had released his name easily enough. "Will he be working a show again soon?" "I don't know. He left in a hurry after the police arrived Thursday and seemed upset by everything." Her smile faltered. "Of course, we all were."

"Is there anything else you can tell me about him?" "Well, he's volunteered for several years and has always been reliable."

"Ever get any complaints about him?"

"Oh no. He's well liked by everyone." Lisa stepped away from Dani, crossing her arms.

"Thank you for your time." Dani turned to see Logan zip up his bag and stand. "I'm going to check something at the box office, then we'll visit Renee's neighborhood."

A man stood behind the counter in the box office. When he finally got off the phone, Dani tried to find out if he knew who had bought Renee's ticket. He claimed not to know and refused to check the computer. Dani bit her lower lip as she backtracked to the main office. The door was locked and the lights off, and no one answered her knock.

"Looks like I'll be back on Monday." Dani pulled her cell phone out of her bag as they reached the Jeep and climbed in. "Do you have Caleb's number on you? Maybe he's made more progress than we have."

Logan rattled it off.

"Thanks." Dani waited for Caleb to answer and frowned when she reached his voice mail. She ended the call and then dialed the station. "Hey, this is Dani. I need Tori. Thanks." Dani slowed while she waited for Tori to pick up. "Tori, I need you to find anything you can on a Michael Stevens. Work your driver's license magic again, 'cause I'd love to see his mug shot." She grinned as Tori screeched about everything on her plate. "Don't worry. I don't need it until five. Thanks."

"You enjoy pushing her buttons, don't you?"

"No more than she pushes mine." She wanted—no, needed—a breakthrough of some sort. She almost whispered a prayer for direction. Instead, she'd knock on doors until she found a neighbor who knew something.

Logan finally pulled into Renee's circle. Dani hopped from the Jeep as he gathered the equipment. Seven houses dotted the circle, and old elm and oak trees shadowed the sidewalk and front yards. The neighborhood bore the feeling of permanence, that it had existed for a long time and would outlast any interlopers. Dani scanned the driveways for cars.

"I'm going to start across the street with the blue house. I'll wave when I need you." Pulling in a steadying breath, Dani smiled and marched across the street. A BMW coupe perched on the driveway, and a child's bike lay in the yard. Dani's heart tightened. Her daughter was old enough to ride one. She climbed the steps to the broad porch and punched the doorbell. Her gaze wandered back to the bike as she waited for an answer. She fought the urge to lean over to see through the window.

The curtain was swept aside, and Dani straightened. She heard a lock release and stepped back as the door opened. A woman peered around the door, toddler nestled against her hip. The sound of other children arguing filtered through the door.

"Can I help you?" The woman jostled the whimpering child.

"I'm Dani Richards with Channel 17, and I wondered if you knew Renee Thomas. She lived across the cul-de-sac from you."

The woman shook her head. "Never heard of her until I saw the headline in today's newspaper."

"She was about my height. A student at the university."

"Nope. Excuse me."

The woman closed the door, and Dani stared at it a moment. She quickly approached the next house, a stately two-story brick. No one answered her knock. As she approached the third house, Dani began to wonder if anyone stayed home on Saturday afternoons.

Dani followed a stone path to the front door. The cherry red door had strips of peeling paint and the flower beds were overgrown with an explosion of crocus and miniature daffodils. A car didn't fill the driveway, but Dani hoped someone would answer. This resident was the most likely to know Renee since the yards' only separation was a low picket fence.

She glanced over her shoulder to check on Logan as she knocked. He stood with crossed legs and arms, his baseball cap pulled over his face. He almost looked as if he could take a nap in that position.

The door opened, and Dani jerked back around.

"Yes?" A woman stood at the door in housecoat and slippers, unconcerned that it was three in the afternoon. A dog-eared *Saturday Evening Post* dangled from one wrinkled hand, and she used the other to push a tuft of gray hair behind her ear. "I'm Dani Richards with—"

"You're that new girl over at Channel 17. Doing a much better job than the young man who left."

"Thank you, ma'am."

"Name's Doris Stone. Don't stand there. Come on in." "All right." Dani followed her tiny hostess down the hallway to the kitchen.

"Have a seat over there. I'll pull some cookies out for us." Doris strode to the fridge and pulled out a small bag of cookies. "I'll slip them in the microwave, and they'll be ready in no time. Would you like some tea?"

Dani hid a smile as the woman bustled to the stove and flipped a switch without waiting for a reply.

"I like mine with cream and sugar. You?"

"Please call me Dani, and that sounds good. Thank you." Doris pulled a mug tree forward on the counter, and grabbed two mugs. Then she pulled out a box of Constant Comment and plopped a tea bag in each cup. "So I suppose you want to hear about Renee."

"Yes. Did you know her?"

"As well as anyone, I suppose. She didn't live here long. Couple months maybe."

"Did you spend any time with her?"

"Not much. It was late winter when she arrived. Too cold and icy for me. I took her a plate of cookies, but she never returned the plate or invited me into her home." Doris sniffed and crossed her arms.

"Did she have many visitors?"

"Not too many. She seemed to stick to herself for the most part when she was home. That wasn't much during the day. But at night there was always some gentleman knocking on the door."

Dani sat up straighter as Doris poured hot water over the tea bags. "Did you recognize him?"

"Oh, there were several. None of them looked familiar, but I didn't study them. I figured it was no business of mine what she did." Doris brought the cups to the table and perched on a chair next to Dani. "She seemed like a nice enough person. No wild parties or anything like that. Just the occasional man at night." "Were there any cars that you saw over and over?" "Honey, I wouldn't know. I'm an old woman who can't see past her front door half the time. How am I supposed to remember what vehicles people drove?" She looked around then popped up from her chair. "Forgot those cookies. Now eat up, this is my mom's secret recipe. So don't bother asking for it." Far from being stale as she'd feared, the cookies melted in Dani's mouth. The sweetness was laced with something tart. She had to ask.

"Don't do it. I'm not going to spill the beans."

"I'll try not to be too disappointed." Dani sipped from the cup. "When was the last time you talked to Renee?"

"Probably a week or so ago. She'd had a box delivered to my house since she knew I'd be home to collect it."

"Do you remember who it was from?"

"No. Just that she was nervous about the contents."

The two chatted a few more minutes. Doris seemed starved for conversation, and Dani enjoyed her stories about matching wits with the contestants on game shows. Finally, noticing the time, Dani jumped up. "Thank you for everything, but I need to run. If you think of anything else, will you call me?" "Only if you promise to stop by for tea."

"I'd be delighted to. Thank you so much."

As soon as the door closed behind her, Dani pulled out her cell phone and tried Caleb's number again. Still no answer. She huffed in frustration, then left a message.

Nothing about this investigation was easy. Working with Caleb only exacerbated the challenge.

10

———

Dani sat in the parking lot, staring at the doors of the nursing home, until the sun's rays lengthened into shadows. Every fiber of her being wanted to race through the doors into the security of Aunt Jayne's embrace, but she sat molded to her seat. Finally, she pushed open her car door and stood. She walked across the parking lot, steps slow. Thursday night had been a good night, but there was no guarantee tonight would be. With Aunt Jayne's early-stage Alzheimer's, more times than not, she didn't recognize Dani.

The strong smell of Lysol permeated the lobby, placing an exclamation point on cleanliness. Muted watercolors lined the beige walls. She wandered to the information booth at the end of the waiting room. An elderly woman with a placid face and tight white curls watched a sitcom. She glanced up as Dani approached.

"May I help you, dear?"

"I'm here to see my aunt, Jayne Richards. Have you seen her?"

"You're that girl from Channel 17, aren't you?" Dani nodded, and the woman lit up like the Christmas tree left in the corner of the room. "Let me see. Dinner's over, a lovely meat loaf and mashed potatoes." The woman's fingers traced a monthly calendar on the desk.

"She's probably in the activity room. If not, let me know. My name is Charlotte."

"Thank you, Charlotte. I'll check there first."

"Glad to help, dear." Charlotte swiveled her chair back toward the TV.

Visits to Aunt Jayne's had stabilized an otherwise chaotic childhood. Her father had avoided Nebraska with any excuse, though usually he relied on work. Her mother dropped her, and disappeared for a month. During that time, Aunt Jayne showered Dani with attention. Picnics for two in the park. Visits to Morrill Hall to view the skeletons of woolly mammoths and other creatures. Sunday services at church filled the weeks.

Dani smiled as the memories wrapped around her like a comforting blanket.

Reaching the first doorway on the left, she peeked into the activity room. A fireplace lined one wall of the cavernous room. An elderly man slept in a kicked back recliner, his snores muffled. Two Ping Pong tables stood with a foosball and air hockey table.

Aunt Jayne hunched over a quilting frame, pushing a needle in and out. The smell of BenGay and peppermint tickled Dani's nose as she walked toward the frame. Lilac and blue fabric squares mixed with yellow triangles in the quilt.

Dani eased up to Aunt Jayne, whose tongue slipped between her lips as she concentrated on her needle. The woman looked up from her work, her face devoid of emotion. "Yes?"

"Hi, Aunt Jayne. It's Dani. I brought your favorite brownies." She held up a container filled with the melt-in-your-mouth treats.

Aunt Jayne's eyes cleared. "Thank you. Where have you been?"

"Can we sit over there and talk?"

Dani led Aunt Jayne to a couch. After getting a cup of warm peppermint tea for each of them, Dani settled next to her. She'd spent countless afternoons in tea parties in Aunt Jayne's dining room.

"What happened to that woman, child?"

"I'm trying to find out." Dani sighed. "Nothing's working yet."

Aunt Jayne caressed Dani's hand with her soft one, and Dani studied the clear veins lining the delicate hand.

"Ask God to lead you to the answers."

"I'm sorry, Aunt Jayne, but I don't think that will work. I've read your Bible the last few nights."

"Lean into its wisdom and get to know its Author, honey. Remember everything you learned in Sunday school? It's all true."

Aunt Jayne's eyes were clear and her expression sincere. The sweet woman honestly believed. In the face of her peace, Dani wished she could, too. "I'll keep reading."

"You won't be disappointed."

Dani smiled, then looked at their interlocked hands. "Aunt Jayne, did anybody ever call in the middle of the night?"

"No. Is something bothering you?"

Dani told Aunt Jayne about the calls, but clouds of confusion drifted into the older woman's eyes. She scooted away from Dani and tapped her toes.

"Do I know you?"

"Aunt Jayne, it's me, Dani."

Puzzlement creased the wrinkles on Aunt Jayne's face.

Dani stood and stepped back. "I'll leave now."

"Where's my quilting? Time's wasting, and Helen needs a wedding present." At her mother's name, Dani's heart sank. Aunt Jayne had traveled twenty-nine years back in time.

Aunt Jayne hummed a hymn under her breath, but ignored Dani. The melody had always been Aunt Jayne's favorite. "Just as I Am, Without One Plea."

She slipped into her car and pulled her phone out. She pushed buttons until the voice mail played. Her stomach clenched at Caleb's voice. He'd finally returned her call, but she didn't like the rush of confusing emotions that the simple sound of his voice brought. She thought she'd killed any emotions tied to him a long time ago. Looked like she couldn't be more wrong.

∽

As his phone rang, Caleb grabbed it and headed out of the conference room so he had a chance of keeping the call. He checked the caller ID and felt a crazy mix of elation and raw fear. Dani had called back, but of course she would since she'd called him first. Yet the past stood between them. She was clearly uncomfortable around him.

Of course, he'd created the elephant in the room when he'd pushed her too hard that late summer evening years ago. She'd reluctantly given him the sex he'd begged for and then withdrew into herself. At the time he hadn't understood why, but had left for college and not thought further. She wasn't the first girl he'd been with, yet Dani had been different. Now since he'd truly turned over his life to the Lordship of Christ, he'd begun to grasp just what he'd done to her. And the thought made his stomach turn.

Taking a deep breath, he clicked a button. "Jamison."

"Hi, Caleb. I missed your call."

The whisper of Dani's words melted something inside him. How did she do it?

"Hello?"

Caleb pulled his thoughts back to the phone. "Sorry about that. Why did you release the victim's name? We're still looking for her parents."

She sighed softly. "I didn't do it. One of the producers took it upon herself. Look, Logan and I were out this afternoon. I talked to a few of Renee's neighbors."

"We've done the same thing." An idea hit him, and he stiffened. "Hey, you want to meet me at Joe's and we can compare notes?"

Silence stretched across the line, and a fist seemed to tighten around his lungs. Must have been too much to ask.

"Maybe... Um... Sure." He could almost see Dani biting her lower lip the way she used to when unsure.

"See you then." He closed the phone and returned to the conference room. "I'm stepping out for a minute. See you in the morning."

Westmont and Denimore didn't bother to look up from their boxes. Caleb slipped away before they could think of something they needed from him. The trip to Joe's took only a few minutes, and he grabbed a table in the corner where he could sit and keep an eye out for Dani. He shot a prayer for wisdom toward heaven. The place was moderately busy for a Saturday night. The aroma of fresh coffee carried the promise of caffeine in large quantities. Light jazz played in the background; his fingers tapped on the table in time to the music.

He looked up and Dani slipped through the door. She'd pulled her long blond hair back in a simple ponytail, and probably didn't realize how much she still looked like the sixteen-year-old he'd fallen in love with. All right, so it had been puppy love, but one look took him back to those days. And nights. He felt heat rise in his face, and hoped she wouldn't notice. He stood and pulled a chair out for her.

"What can I get for you?"

"How about a small cafe mocha. Better make it decaf." Her nose crinkled.

"I'll be right back." Caleb wondered what she'd uncovered that had her calling him. Dani looked so small huddled at the table. Whatever it was, he hoped he could remove the burden from her. He grabbed the finished drinks, a stack of napkins and the cookies, and headed to the table. "Here you go, Dani."

She smiled as she lifted the cup and sniffed the aroma. "Thanks. I hope you don't expect me to eat any of those cookies."

Caleb examined the bite-size mix of cookies, wondering what was wrong with them. "Why not?"

"You don't spend your life in front of the camera, which adds ten pounds."

"I don't think you have anything to worry about. You look great to me. So have one."

She blushed and looked away. She seemed to settle some- thing in her mind and reached for a yellow cookie that might be lemon.

"So..."

"I think I have the usher's name for you. See what you can learn about Michael Stevens."

"Why do you think that's his name?"

"Let's just say I have my sources." He quirked an eyebrow, and she grimaced. "Fine. They had an usher policy meeting at the Lied today.

He wasn't there, but the coordinator thought it could be him." She took a sip of her mocha and leaned back. "I also talked to one of Renee's neighbors. That woman thought Renee had a lot of men going in and out. She also accepted a package for Renee a week before she died. Thought Renee was pretty worked up about whatever was in it." "Okay. I'll follow up on both of those. Which neighbor was this?"

"Doris Stone."

"Right. The nextdoor neighbor."

Dani sat back. "That's it. What do you have for me?" "Not much. Looks like we've been talking to the same people. We're also trying to figure out her research." He chuckled as Dani shuddered. "Denimore agrees with you. Thinks it's indecipherable."

"Professor Bartholomew indicated her work was solid, even breakthrough material. He thought there might be a problem with her fellowship though."

"Have you followed up on that angle?"

"Not yet. Her faculty sponsor is out of the country and hard to reach."

"And the fellowship donor is out of town." Caleb considered his next words, then leaned forward, elbows on the table. "When are we going to talk about us? Dani, there's still a lot between us."

She crossed her arms and looked away. He waited, but she'd gone mute. Her chin wobbled, and he frantically looked around for a napkin. "Don't cry, Dani. Please."

She clamped her lips together, and swiped a hand across her eyes. She grabbed her coffee and stood. Caleb scrambled to his feet.

"Thanks for the coffee." Dani scurried from the table and out the door.

Caleb watched her go, wondering what had happened. The sinking feeling in his gut confirmed things hadn't gone well at all.

11

With a groan, Dani dragged a pillow over her head. She couldn't get Caleb out of her mind. After years of training her mind to ignore her heart, now she could only imagine what her life would look like if she'd told him everything. That she was pregnant. Would he have asked her to marry him? Would their daughter be with them now, rather than living with strangers? Would she feel the security of his love? Or would he resent the fact that she'd forced responsibility on him? That she hadn't somehow prevented the pregnancy?

Dani flipped onto her stomach and took a couple deep breaths. She tried to think of anything but Caleb as she waited for sleep to come. The distant ring of the telephone pulled at her dreams. She struggled with the sheets entwined around her legs. Giving up, she slapped her hand along the top of the nightstand until her fingers wrapped around the clock. Pulling it toward her, she groaned. Only 2:30 a.m., and sleep would be slow to return.

Maybe the caller had a message that couldn't wait until a reasonable time. She was on call for breaking news, so she threw the clock to the floor and grabbed the phone. So much for a good night's sleep. "Hello?"

Silence flowed from the phone.

"Is someone there? Do you know what time it is?" Her voice rose.

"Stop the investigation. You didn't listen the last time I called. Tomorrow you won't be so lucky." Dani shuddered and slammed the phone back in place. She'd heard of viewers stalking members of the media, but this was crazy. She hurried to the office to grab a notepad and jot down the words.

Dani closed her eyes after returning to bed, but sleep refused to return. The minutes ticked away, and it became clear she was too awake to trick her mind into sleep. Stuffing a pillow behind her back, she grabbed the Bible. She began to read in the Psalms. Peace flowed into her as she read.

In the morning, Dani examined the circles under her eyes. After pulling on her jogging outfit, she rummaged along the top of her desk for the Lincoln street map.

She needed exercise, and refused to use a treadmill. It reminded her too much of a hamster trapped on a wheel, going nowhere. She settled on the university's city campus. Dani refolded the map, then headed to her car.

She glanced at the answering machine and its blinking message light. The calls must have come while she got ready. She hit the play button. Nothing but heavy breathing sliced the room.

She hit skip. More heavy breathing. She reached for the delete button reflexively, but couldn't punch it. Not until she knew more, though logic told her a tape of heavy breathing wouldn't help Caleb. Once in the car, she turned the radio up and sang along with the country song. Anything to drown the words of the early morning call.

Pulling into a spot vacated by a student, Dani braced for a run. The weather was perfect, and the campus's wide sidewalks made an ideal location. She checked her shoelaces, inserted her small earphones and started down the sidewalk.

The upbeat music set a good pace and kept her moving. Leaf buds hinted at blossoms ready to open. She pushed the investigation to the background of her mind. If this case was anything like others, her subconscious needed to work on it awhile. If only the caller didn't make it so personal. She opened and closed her hands, trying to deflect the creeping tension.

Findley Hall came into view, and Dani slowed. Had Renee jogged around campus? Did her murderer know her through the university? Dani glanced at her watch and switched direction, picking up her pace. Twenty minutes meant she'd circled campus for two miles.

Even on a late Sunday morning campus vibrated with vitality. The mild spring day had pulled students from their frat houses and dorms. They clustered in the center of campus soaking in the sunshine.

She slowed to a walk and surveyed downtown. Lincoln's status as Nebraska's state capital and home to the Cornhusker football team bracketed the skyline. The state capitol towered over the skyline, opposite the stadium's large red *N*.

Time to head home. An empty afternoon faced her, but she'd tackle the boxes stacked around her house. When she reached the house, Dani opened the back gate. Something white fluttered on her door. Dani hurried up the steps. The tape's grip nearly ripped the note in half as she pulled it off the door. Once in the kitchen, she opened the message on the island countertop.

Large block letters marched across the sheet. The hair on the back of her neck prickled. She picked up the note, as if a closer look would change the words. "You should be more careful, little girl..."

This was no friendly message. Dani swallowed hard, and the paper fluttered from her fingers. She felt so cold. So alone. He'd found her home.

CARS ZIPPED along Vine Street as Caleb sat on Dani's front porch late Sunday morning. People had forgotten how to soak in a day of peace. He wasn't sure why he waited at her door when he should be at the precinct or resting.

Caleb doubted Dani would leap at the chance to spend the afternoon with him. The past and his mistakes hung like a steel curtain between them. She had such an edge, and he wanted to remove his contribution to it. He'd headed toward the precinct, but came here instead.

Two boys played across the street. Caleb watched them for a moment before heading to his car. This was crazy. He should call her, set up a time to see her. If she'd let him. The sound of a gate slamming reached him and he hesitated. Maybe she was back. He might be crazy, but he had to check.

He hurried up the front steps. Someone had parted the front curtains at Dani's, so he knocked on the door. He glanced through the window as he waited. After a minute, he knocked again. He heard her clomping down the wooden stairs before he saw her. When she opened the front door, Caleb stepped back. Her face reflected the white walls behind her. As she swayed he reached out to steady her. She cringed and jerked away from his touch.

"What are you doing here?" Her voice rose to a shriek.

The words wailed from her mouth before she could stifle them. "Why are you here? Go away. Please." She ground the words out. She needed to be alone. Collect herself.

Even as she tried to pull away, Caleb pushed his way inside and led her to the couch.

"Dani, talk to me. What's wrong?"

She wanted to believe the concern in his eyes. Why care now? "Please leave."

"Dani, I'll leave. But you have to tell me what happened first."

She looked down at her hands. Watched her fingers flutter around her lap until she grasped them together. Even then they twisted together, a mirror image of her thoughts.

"I'll be right back." Caleb left the living room.

She heard him open and close cabinet doors, looking for something. The world closed in as she struggled to keep her bearings. How had he found her? She stilled her hands, but felt her body rock back and forth like a metronome. Control. She must find it or Caleb would probe with too many questions and leave her no choice but to answer.

Dani jumped as Caleb thrust a glass of water at her.

"Have a drink. Then we'll talk."

Dani took the glass and watched the ice cubes dance in the water. They seemed so free even though they were trapped in a small space. Caleb settled on the love seat across from Dani. After giving her a moment, he straightened, and Dani stifled a groan. Inquisition time. The questions might be gentle, but the intent remained the same. Pull information from her.

"I never should have moved here." The words eased out, soft in the quiet room. "I can still sense her here."

"Jayne?"

Dani nodded and set the glass on the end table. "I moved here to help her, you know. By the time I got this job, my family had moved her into an assisted living home."

"If she needs help, your schedule isn't the best for that."

"Maybe. But I could have found in-home help." Dani studied her hands.

"Dani, why were you as white as your house when you opened the door?"

She fought the urge to get up and leave the room. No matter where she went, he'd follow. Persistence was too ingrained in his personality.

"Dani?" The concern in his eyes couldn't be faked. She felt her defenses melt away.

"A note. It was on the back door when I got home." Her body tensed as she remembered the feeling. "I went jogging on campus." She flashed a crooked smile. "When I got home, I found a note taped to the back door. I didn't think anything of it, though I should have." She stopped as the words seared in her mind played like a tape. *You should be more careful, little girl. Campus on a Sunday is empty. Don't ever forget I'm watching you.*

"Where's the note, Dani?"

"Over there." She waved a hand toward the stairs.

"Show me. Then we're getting out of here for a bit. Can you get ready to leave in ten minutes?"

Dani nodded and headed up the stairs, Caleb close behind her. She heard him pull out his cell phone and call another officer while he walked. She fought the urge to bristle as Caleb, with his calm air, took control of the situation. All she wanted to do was curl up—in privacy— and evaluate her options.

Feeling Caleb's gaze, Dani lifted her chin and turned toward her desk. Papers covered the surface and appeared to be a mishmash of clutter. However, the note blinked like a neon sign. She reached to take it from the top pile, but her fingers refused to pick it up.

Caleb brushed her back as he leaned in and picked up the paper. She was startled to see a glove on his hand. He held up the message. "Do you have something I can slip this into?"

She nodded and retrieved an envelope from the file cabinet.

"Tell me if anything else happens." Caleb slipped the envelope into his back jeans pocket. "More notes. Phone calls. Messages on the answering machine. You can't handle this on your own." He turned toward her and crossed his arms. "I can't help if I don't know what's happening."

12

Dani's heart skipped a beat, and she held her breath. She wanted to step away, put some distance between them, stop the tingles that chased up and down her spine. A rush of heat flooded her cheeks under his scrutiny. Why wouldn't he leave? If he stayed, she'd tell him about the calls, and she'd rather tell any of the other officers. She couldn't depend on Caleb. Not when he'd abandoned her before.

"I'm not leaving until you tell me everything."

"I want to stay here, figure out what's next in this investigation." She couldn't risk more time with Caleb. She had to protect herself before her heart shattered again.

"Get changed or whatever you need." He stepped closer and chucked her chin.

The intensity in his gaze had warnings blaring in her mind. They were getting too close, way too soon. There was so much Caleb didn't know yet. Dani scuttled around him and rushed across the hall to the bathroom. She closed the door and locked it, glad for the space. The woman in the mirror looked confused, almost lost.

Dani tried to focus on the note and what to do about it. Her thoughts returned to the tall investigator waiting in her office. Being alone with Caleb created a war inside her. Much as she hated to admit it, he still stirred emotions in her.

As she towel dried her hair, she decided she had to trust him. He was the officer in charge of the investigation. Ten years was a long time. Maybe he'd changed as much as she had.

CALEB WATCHED Dani slip across the hall. He rubbed his hands over his head and groaned. He had a lot of ground to cover to make things right with her. He just prayed she'd give him the chance to explain. The more time he spent with her, the more his thoughts returned to her and the future he wanted for them.

The muffled sound of water running filtered through the door. He hoped his plan didn't backfire. It felt like a winner. He hoped she agreed. Either way it was too late to back out. While he waited, he called Denimore. "I've got a note for you to pick up. Meet me at Dani Richards's."

Caleb studied the office as he waited for Denimore and Dani. No other documents looked like they had anything to do with the Thomas murder. So why was Dani so tense? Sure, the note had been taped to her door, but there had to be more going on. Whether she liked it or not, she had to tell him. He was the lead officer on this case, and as such, she was his responsibility as a witness. Dani definitely wouldn't like it, but there was nothing he could do about that.

A pounding on the door echoed up the hallway as the water turned off. Caleb left the office and opened the door for Denimore. "Come on in. We've got some more work to do."

"Anything that will give us a lead?"

"Not sure." He handed the envelope to Denimore. "This was left on Dani's door while she was out. Whoever left it knew where she was. Followed her to campus, then beat her home. She's pretty spooked."

"This the first note?"

"Yes, but I'm sure something else is going on. We'll find out when she comes downstairs."

"So maybe whoever left the note is tied in with the Thomas murder."

Caleb rubbed his hands over his head. "It's possible." Until he knew for sure, he'd stick close to Dani.

"Here's hoping there's a connection. We need one." Denimore straightened, and Caleb looked up the stairs.

She had no idea how beautiful she was. Today, without the makeup and tailored clothes she usually wore, she turned his head. He liked this simpler Dani in jeans and a teal turtleneck that matched her eyes. This Dani reminded him of the girl he'd loved ten years earlier.

"Mr. Denimore." Dani looked up at Caleb, questions filling her eyes.

"Why don't we get a drink in the kitchen?" He and Denimore headed down the hallway, Dani trailing behind. "Dani, you have to fill us in on everything. What else is happening besides this note?"

She squared her jaw and stared at him. "What makes you think anything is?"

"You were too upset when you opened the door for the note alone."

"Miss Richards, we can't help if you don't tell us the whole story. If anything's tied to the Thomas murder, we need it."

Dani eyed Denimore, then shrugged. "You're going to think I have an overactive imagination." She pulled out a drawer on the island and pulled out a small tape. "I'm getting calls. Odd ones. I don't know what to make of them. Some have messages, but only if I pick up. Those that go to the answering machine are filled with silence." She tossed Caleb the tape. "That's what's on here. Nothing but silence."

"How often are the calls coming?"

"When I'm out, I can get six or seven messages. In the middle of the night, I might get one or two calls. Just enough to keep me from sleeping."

Denimore slipped the tape into his jacket pocket. "What does this man say in the calls?"

"Stop the investigation."

"Or what?"

"Or I won't be so lucky." Dani grimaced. "Like I could feel lucky with this monster out there shadowing me."

"Is there anything else you aren't telling us, Dani?" Caleb searched her eyes, but nothing seemed hidden in her expression.

"Isn't that enough? He leaves notes at my house. He calls at all hours. I don't know what to do, but I'm not letting him scare me off the investigation."

Fine, but she'd find Caleb glued to her side as much as the investigation allowed. And when he couldn't be there, he'd make sure Logan was. He had to keep her safe.

Denimore stood. "All right. I'll get this tape and the letter back to the office for processing. See if we can't get something off of them."

"Let me know as soon as you find something."

"Will do. Goodbye, Miss Richards."

Dani walked Denimore to the door. After he left, she stood there holding the door. "Aren't you leaving, too?"

"Nope. I've got a surprise, one I think you'll enjoy."

Caleb helped her into his car. After fifteen quiet minutes he pulled up to a small brick building and tapped Dani on the shoulder.

She blinked. "Why are we at an animal shelter?"

"I've thought about getting a dog. Maybe you can help me find the perfect canine."

"I don't know about that." While her tone was reluctant, she followed him with a bounce in her step. "I've thought about getting a cat."

"Why?"

"I talk to myself at home. Rather than a roommate I might despise, I'll get a cat that won't talk back."

"How about a dog?"

"No, thanks. Too much work."

"We'll start there. See what I can find."

Dani followed him into the loud room. In the third kennel, a black Lab mix sat, eyes on them. Dani stepped in front of him.

"If you got a dog and hated it, I could always take it."

No matter which animal they looked at, she kept returning to the black Lab mix named Job. At a year, he'd reached full size and teetered on the side of maturity with plenty of puppy sparks left to keep life interesting.

She looked up from the floor, Job curled next to her. "I think he's the one."

"All right. Let's complete the paperwork and get him home." After a stop for dog food, he pulled into the alley. Job jumped from the car and pulled him toward the fence. Caleb eyed the short picket fence. "Job's bigger than I thought. I hope this fence is high enough to contain him."

"Don't worry. I'll call you every time he escapes to chase something." Dani juggled several bags of pet toys and food as she walked up the back steps.

After Dani dumped her burdens on the counter, she sat on a bar stool. Caleb leaned against the counter and watched Job sniff around the first floor. As Dani laughed at Job's antics, Caleb watched her more than Job. "It was worth a month's salary in dog food to hear you laugh like that. You've always had a beautiful laugh."

Color tinted her cheeks as she met his gaze. "Well, it's easy to laugh with him clowning around."

Caleb chuckled. "Let me know if you need anything." As Job slid past Dani on the hardwood floors, Caleb squeezed her arm. "I'll let myself out. Sleep well."

Dani nodded then turned her attention to Job as he plopped at her feet.

Maybe Denimore had found something with the note or tape. As he headed to the police station, Caleb hoped for good news. He needed some before the game turned deadly and Dani was the next victim.

13

M onday morning Dani awoke bleary-eyed. Job had howled sometime in the wee hours of dawn when the phone rang. She'd been desperate for a good night's sleep, so she thought she'd turned off all the ringers. She must have missed one. Now she was paying the price. Her morning meeting was not going to be fun, especially since the drive to work failed to pep her up.

"Glad you could join us." Kate nailed her with a glare over the top of her tiny bifocals as Dani seated herself in the last chair at the conference table. "You're up. What are your plans for this week?"

"Logan and I got some great interviews Saturday that I'll follow up on today. We'll also turn those into some fresh packages for tonight's shows. I should wrap up the investigation this week." Dani found Logan across the table. "I'll need Logan through Wednesday or Thursday."

Tori rolled her eyes from her seat across the table. "Must be nice to think you can focus exclusively on one story. Is that how they did it in St. Louis?"

"Come on, Tori. She's chasing the biggest story in Lincoln." Phil

Baker smoothed his tie into place as Dani looked at him, surprised by his defense. What did he have up his sleeve?

Phil turned his attention back to Kate. "Sounds like you didn't relax enough this weekend. You'll have to join me at Branched Oak next week." He pasted a placid smile on his lips. "Nothing's better than a weekend at the cabin. Are we done?"

A tinge of color climbed Kate's cheeks. With anyone else, the color reflected rage. But with Phil, it tilted toward pleasure. His hold on Kate buzzed through the newsroom, but the woman seemed oblivious.

"All right, folks, go find the news. We've got newscasts to fill. Dani, I need you."

Dani sipped a Dr Pepper and waited for the room to empty. Eventually, the only other person there was Kate, who leaned across the table.

"You're a great reporter, Dani, but I'm concerned. Your professionalism is slipping and I can't let that affect your projects." Kate swirled her coffee around her mug. "Frankly, with your experience, I expect more."

"Come on, Kate. It was only a couple minutes."

"Try thirty. You can't be late to interviews and appointments."

"I'm not. But if I don't leave and work the phone, I might be."

"Make sure it doesn't happen again."

Dani grabbed her soda and bolted from the table. "Thanks for the pep talk, Kate."

When she reached her cube, Logan grinned at her from the chair. "Caleb told me about your adventure. How's Job?"

"Just dandy. I'm late because good ole Job barked half the night."

Logan frowned at her. "Why?"

"No one was prowling, Logan. Just more calls, and Job took it as an excuse to bark. Maybe he likes a full moon. Remind me to say no the next time Caleb surprises me." Dani reached for her phone and motioned Logan away. "Can I have my chair? I have calls to make before we head out." Logan waved her to his seat. "I'll load my gear. Page when you're ready."

She looked through the campus directory numbers for food science grad students. Finding one, she dialed the number and listened as the phone rang. When voice mail picked up, she left a short message requesting a callback and then moved down the list to the next name. After leaving several more messages she finally reached a student willing to meet with her in an hour. Enough time to stop by the box office first.

Rather than page Logan, she grabbed her purse and briefcase. She headed to the Jeep and found Logan waiting. "Let's go—we're headed to Findley Hall."

"Aye aye, Captain." Logan pulled out of the parking lot and headed toward campus.

Dani turned on the radio. A country song filled the van, and she turned down the volume. "I've got to get you some better music."

"Stick around and you'll become a fan."

She crinkled her nose at the thought. "Not in this lifetime. I want to stop by the box office at the Lied first."

Logan parked in a lot between the Lied Center and Findley. Dani hurried to the box office. After entering the building, she pounded on a locked door that led to the back.

A moment later, a kid with long brown hair tied in a ponytail appeared at the window. "Can I help you?" His nasally voice echoed through the grate.

"Yes. I have a couple quick questions. Do you work the ticket window often?"

"Monday to Friday between one and four."

"Great. Then you can help me. Do you know who purchased the tickets for Renee Thomas's box?"

He rolled his eyes like it was the dumbest question. "Yes, but I've already told the cops and I can't tell you."

"Look, young man, I found Miss Thomas, and I will investigate until I find her killer." She slowed down. He didn't want to know the details. "Please tell me who bought the tickets." "I guess it's not a secret. That local TV guy, Phil somebody, bought them."

"Phil Baker?" Dani's jaw dropped at the name.

He shrugged and looked at her through his vintage frames. "That sounds right. I think he bought 'em, but someone else picked them up."

"Who was that?"

"A young girl. She looked like you. Blonde, green eyes. A looker. The tickets were already paid for and she asked for his."

"So anyone who knew he bought the tickets could have collected them at the window ?"

"I suppose."

"You don't require photo "ID?" Dani didn't try to hide her disbelief.

"Well..." Reddish color climbed the young man's neck, and he looked away.

"I thought you said you worked afternoons."

"Sometimes I help on show nights, too." A phone rang, and he quickly picked it up.

Dani waited a minute, but he closed the window and turned his back. So much for helpful customer service. She rushed back to the sidewalk where Logan waited. He started to say something, and she shook her head. "I'll tell you later. I need a little more time to think about what I just learned. And we have thirty minutes to reach the student who agreed to talk to us, before she leaves." Dani raced up Findley's steps, trusting Logan was behind her. They rode the elevator to the ninth floor. "She said she was this way."

Pay dirt. She felt her pulse race when she read the nameplates next to the door. Renee had shared this office with Laurel Buchanan. Dani rapped on the door and poked her head inside the small office. Two desks were pushed against opposite walls; the chaos spilling from one and encroaching on the painful neatness of the other. A tall redhead sat at the latter. She looked up and smiled.

"You must be the reporter."

"Dani Richards. And this is my photographer, Logan Collins. Do you mind if he sets up and tapes our conversation?" "That should be okay. Please come in." She looked around the tight space. "I suppose you can sit at Renee's desk." "Thanks." They made small talk for the few minutes it took Logan to get everything set up. Logan finally signaled he was ready. "Laurel, could you spell your name for me?" Dani waited as Laurel spelled it for the camera. "I'm sitting at Renee's desk, right? Has anyone been through Renee's desk yet?"

"Just a police investigator. Her parents are supposed to come to town sometime this week. I wanted to leave it as is until then."

Dani nodded. Small comfort for her family to go through it. It would take more than that to bring any closure. She pulled out her notebook of questions. "How long have you known Renee?"

"Since she arrived on campus in the fall."

"Did you have any classes together?"

"No. Our areas of emphasis are...were different. She looked at food safety and bioterrorism, while I'm more on the food development side. New flavors for sports drinks, things like that."

"Did you do things together outside of this office?"

"Not too much. Renee was a loner. She preferred dates to girls' nights. She always had a boyfriend or two that she spent most of her time with." Laurel reached up to a shelf over her desk and pulled down a framed photo. "Here's a photo of us at a faculty mixer. It was one of the few things she'd go to. See this guy behind her? They dated for a few months, but I never got the sense they were too committed. Then they broke up at Christmas, but just in the last couple weeks things seemed to get hot again."

"Can I see that?"

"Sure."

Dani reached for the photo and carefully examined it. Renee looked happy and relaxed in designer jeans and a buttondown shirt. "Do you know what his name is?"

"Reed Donovan. He's a Ph.D. student in engineering, I think."

"Not exactly an overlap."

"You'd be surprised. I think they met initially when she needed help on her fellowship project." Her shoulders slumped. "Now we'll never know how far she could have taken that."

"Did she and Reed fight?"

"Oh, no. He brought her flowers last Tuesday. Tulips. It made her week." Laurel's face sagged as if she hadn't slept since Renee's murder. "She was visibly happy for the first time all year. She stopped taking calls from other boyfriends. She'd decided Reed was the one.

"She enjoyed flirting...a lot. One guy this year was more serious than the rest. She pulled out all the stops to get him. Then strung him along. She had a way about her that attracted all kinds."

"Do you know this last guy's name?"

"No. She was careful about his calls. Only on her cell phone. And that got sporadic service here. She got so excited when he called. She always called him back."

"Anything else you can tell us about Renee?"

Laurel came to life as she talked about Renee's research and personality. "She was a wonderful gal I enjoyed working with. She had too much to live for." Just as quickly, a mask fell on her face, stiffening her features.

CALEB GAZED AT THE WHITEBOARD, arms akimbo. "Hey, Denimore, is Cornelius back in town yet?"

"The fellowship guy? Supposed to return last night."

"All right. I think Westmont and I'll pay him a visit." He grabbed the Cornelius file. The folder didn't contain much information beyond his address and business profile. He tapped Westmont on the shoulder. "You get to drive."

Caleb had expected Cornelius to live in the old money section of town. Many of Lincoln's entrepreneurs congregated in the stately brick homes situated in neighborhoods clustered on either side of Forty-eighth Street. Instead, he'd chosen a newer section of town on the far south side. As the view morphed from old neighborhoods to strip malls and then to subdivisions layered on top of subdivisions, Caleb reviewed the scant info in the file. He'd have his work cut out for him in the interview.

"Did you check to see if he'd be home this morning?" Westmont talked around a wad of gum.

"His secretary assured me he's not at the office and won't be until afternoon."

"Here we are."

Westmont pulled in front of a rambling two-story home. Immature trees and shrubs dotted the yard leading to the stucco monstrosity. The home looked modern and cold. A long walk led them to the front door. Caleb squared his shoulders and pressed the doorbell. Its gong echoed through the door.

A woman in her late thirties opened the door. Soft lines etched her face as she smiled, revealing her to be older than her youthful tennis outfit indicated. "Hello? Can I help you?"

Caleb pulled out his badge. "I'm Investigator Jamison and this is Officer Westmont with the Lincoln police. Is Mr. Cornelius home?"

She tilted her head and studied the badges. "Why do you need Roger?"

"We'd like to learn more about his fellowship at the university."

"Come in, and I'll see if he's available." The woman stepped aside, and Caleb and Westmont followed her into a sweeping entryway. The two-story ceilings soared above Caleb's head and pulled his attention toward the windows lining the opposite wall. The groomed yard blended into a golf course fairway.

Caleb wandered to a wall lined with built-in bookshelves. Row after row of texts guarded one section of classics. "I think I found one book I've read."

"Then you've missed many excellent volumes." A deep voice carried across the room.

Caleb turned to see a compact man enter the room. "Mr. Cornelius, thank you for seeing us. I'm Investigator Jamison."

"Yes. And this is Officer Westmont. Please, have a seat." Energy flowed from him as he sank onto a leather couch. He adjusted the pleats in his pressed khakis. "How can I help Lincoln's finest today?"

Caleb leaned forward from his perch on a suede couch. "Mr.

Cornelius, tell me about your fellowship at the university. Why did you create it?"

Cornelius explained he'd wanted to pay back the university that launched his career by helping students with tuition costs. As he'd talked to staff, he'd been intrigued with the idea that he could direct research toward his company's needs.

"In the last seven years, we've realized how vulnerable our food systems are. We need to protect the food supply without adding prohibitive cost. Irradiation is one way to kill organisms that might be injected to food, but it won't work in all circumstances."

"Is that what the fellows studied this year?"

Cornelius nodded, then leaned back. "You should understand that even though they all receive the fellowship, I also set up a competition. Each year I award an additional sum to the graduate student who develops a system or product my business can utilize immediately."

Caleb looked up from his notes. "What was the contest this year?"

"Developing an alternative system to irradiation for beef. Many producers would benefit."

"Are they making progress?"

"I receive occasional updates unless a problem or spectacular success occurs." He paused and lifted his glasses from his nose before wiping a line of sweat away. "Look. Renee Thomas had interesting early results. I'm sure you know we met for lunch occasionally to discuss them. There was nothing more to our relationship."

"Did anyone join the two of you for the lunches?"

"No. They focused on business. Renee's passion for her research was contagious. I've worn a management hat long enough. It was an escape to hear about hands-on research for a change."

They talked for a few more minutes, but Cornelius didn't add any new information. Caleb reviewed his notes, then looked at Westmont, who shook his head. Caleb tucked his notebook back in his inside jacket pocket.

"Thank you for your time. Will you be in town if we have more questions?"

Cornelius bobbed his head. He straightened his pleats as he stood. "Now, if you'll excuse me. Business beckons." Caleb watched him hustle from the room. He got the sense more existed between Cornelius and Renee, but the man had skirted the subject like a pro.

14

Dani opened her eyes as Logan pulled into the station's parking lot. She touched up her lipstick and climbed from the vehicle. Another deadline loomed, made even tighter by their futile search for Renee's boyfriend, Reed Donovan. They'd found more grad students who'd known Renee. According to them, she'd been incredibly smart and threw her all into everything.

Dani's breath hitched while her mind raced with ways to structure the story. "I'll draft the package. Review the video for background video. I'll pick a couple sound bites. We'll turn them into a package for the five-thirty show."

Dani hurried to bay 3. She popped the tape and pulled on the headphones. She scanned Laurel Buchanan's interview at chipmunk speed. Dani noted the sound bite she wanted, and rewound the interview. She listened carefully at normal speed. Laurel's bite would come at the end of the package.

Logan tapped her shoulder making her jump.

"Ready for me?"

"Use bites one, three, five and six. Tell Tori she'll have a two minute usher reaction story for five-thirty. The shorter student piece can air on a later newscast." She handed him the notebook with the quotes highlighted.

Dani returned to her desk. She drafted the usher piece, then ran to the booth and recorded the audio. Throwing the tape of her voice-over at Logan, she drafted what Phil would read on camera.

This afternoon students had mixed reactions to the Thursday murder of Renee Thomas. One of their own, Renee studied food manufacturing processes and was developing innovative ways to protect our nation's food system. The fact a student was murdered didn't bother Jason Patelli... Cut to sound bite... Another student felt compelled to issue a warning to the residents of Lincoln... Cut to sound bite... Back to Phil on camera two... At this time, police are no closer to publicly identifying a suspect.

The phone on her desk rang, and she grabbed it.

"Hello?"

"Hey, Dani." Caleb's voice slid across the line. "What are you doing tonight?"

"Heading home. That dog you talked me into needs to go outside."

"Want company?" He'd hesitated between words, almost as if rethinking the offer.

Under the intensity of the silence, Dani wanted to squirm like a child put on the spot by a difficult question. "I just want to relax tonight. I'm desperate to catch up on my sleep."

He sighed, and she could hear the longing in that sigh. Silence stretched as she waited a moment. She could see Logan across the room. "I have to go."

"We're not done, Dani."

"Goodbye." Dani eased the phone back before he could say anything else and darted toward Logan. At the edit bay, she focused on the story. When it ended, she gave Logan a thumbs up. "Looks great as always. On to the ten o'clock package." The second package wrote itself and within half an hour she handed the tape with her audio to Logan. She looked at the wall clock hanging over the edit bays. "See you in the morning." She slipped her car from its spot. She frowned at a thumping sound and pulled the car into park. Stepping from the vehicle, she turned and gasped. Both tires on the driver's side were flat. She edged around to the other side and found those tires equally flat.

Dani sank to the ground, her mind racing. Who would slash her tires? Did anyone see who did this? The parking lot usually had a lot of activity as people came and went on assignment. She opened her phone and found the address book on the second try. She dialed Caleb and pulled herself up. Her legs shook so much she leaned against the car to keep from sliding back down.

"Dani?"

"I need you. Now." Her teeth chattered. She couldn't force another word out.

"Where are you?" Caleb's voice pitched in the way it used to when he was concerned.

"Work parking lot."

"Get back in the building. I'll be there in five minutes." "Okay." Dani eyed the distance. Was anyone hiding in the shadows, waiting for her?

"I want to know Logan's there."

"I see him."

"Good."

"Why?"

"Let's just call it history. He's the only one I trust to take care of you until I get there. I'll be there in five minutes," he repeated. "Stay put." The sound of a door slamming echoed before the call ended.

Slashed tires were a dangerous step up from notes and calls. Dani sank into a chair in the empty lobby. She stared at the phone. She should do something. Call Triple A. Arrange for a rental car. *What next?* After the next attack, would someone call an ambulance for her?

CALEB FLIPPED the lights on his vehicle and zipped between cars in the moderate traffic on Twenty-seventh Street.

How could he protect Dani when she continued to push him away any time he tried to help her? Hopefully now she'd take the calls and notes seriously. Whoever sent them had moved to a new level. *Lord, keep her safe.* He whipped onto Vine, and prayed until he pulled into the Channel 17 parking lot.

The lobby lights were on when he entered. Logan knelt in front of a chair that Dani slumped in. An urge to push Logan away from Dani flashed through Caleb. That was crazy. He'd asked Logan to keep her company. He hadn't meant that close though. At least Dani didn't look too receptive to the extra attention. Though she wasn't any more welcoming when he was the one near her. Someday he'd make it up to her in a way she could understand.

Caleb cleared his throat, and Dani turned to him. Her face looked pale, and there was a tightness and fragility to her expression. She could shatter at any moment. "Thanks for waiting with her, Logan."

"No problem." Logan jumped to his feet and moved into the doorway.

Caleb strode to Dani and sat across from her. "What happened?"

"Someone slashed all my tires. I didn't notice until I tried to leave a bit ago." She grabbed a breath and froze. "He knows where I work."

"Of course he does, Dani. Most of Lincoln knows that."

Dani rubbed her hands up and down her arms and rocked slightly on the couch. Caleb longed to slip onto the couch next to her. Hold her until the fear left. Only Logan eyeing them from the doorway kept him frozen in place.

"I'll call the techs to come look at your car." He hesitated. "You're not sleeping at home tonight. Any thoughts on where you'd like to go?"

"Is St. Louis an option?" She smiled weakly, and he had to admire the flash of humor.

"A bit of a distance for solving this case."

"Where would you recommend? I'm not going home with you."

"Maybe Tricia is home. If not, I'll find an alternative." Her stormy look made him brace for a fight. When she was silent, he handed the phone back to her. "Let's get you out of here."

Dani tilted her chin and left the building with her head high. Caleb settled her in the passenger side of his car. "Still like cheese Runzas?"

"Only if you order some onion rings and a smoothie, too. Mango banana for me."

Okay, her appetite had returned. That was a good sign. He took her to a Runza drive-through and ordered two of each item. In a few minutes they and the comforting warm bags of food were climbing the back steps to her house. "Wait here while I sweep the house."

She rolled her eyes, but let him lead her into the house. He worked his way through the rooms on the first floor, then the basement, and finally upstairs. The sound of dishes clanking against each other chased him through the house. She must have entered the kitchen despite his instructions. Job trailed his steps with a droop to his tail. Almost as if he was offended Caleb thought he'd let somebody in.

He circled back to the kitchen. Dani stared at the answering machine and chewed her lower lip. She'd set the island with plates and spread the Runzas and rings across them. The yeasty aroma teased him, but he grabbed a ring then stepped behind Dani and looked at the machine. The digital display flashed. He pressed play, and stilled when Dani leaned into him.

A heavy breather left the first message. In the second, Tricia, Caleb's sister, asked if she and Dani could get together. He smiled as he listened to that one. Tricia was never one to miss an opportunity to renew a friendship. The third message crackled. "Better listen next time or worse things will happen to you." The voice was garbled and indistinct. Caleb hit replay and leaned in closer to the machine.

If he had anything to do with it, Dani wouldn't be alone until he found the person slashing her tires and leaving these messages.

Now if he could only get her to cooperate.

15

Dani's stomach growled as the tangy aroma of onion rings filled the kitchen. She dipped one in ketchup, eyeing Caleb as she ate. The set of his jaw as he listened to the message—again—worried her.

He reached to hit the replay button, but she grabbed his hand. "The message won't change."

"But maybe I'll catch a nuance I've missed." Worry clouded his eyes.

"Then take the machine. For now, eat while the food's hot and the smoothies haven't melted."

Caleb ran his hands over his head, then settled on the stool next to her. "Does the message mean anything to you?" "Only that I've ticked someone off."

"Enough to slash your tires. Leave notes on your door. Call you."

Dani shuddered. "But slashing the tires didn't hurt me. I can replace the tires. The calls, note, all of it has to connect with stopping my Renee Thomas investigation. Why, I don't have a clue. We aren't making much progress."

"Who do you think is behind this?"

"I don't know. The usher? But I have no idea why."

"I'm not going to sleep well until I know this case is wrapped up and you're safe."

Dani grabbed the Runza and took a bite. Runzas were a completely Nebraskan experience she'd loved from the first bite. She sipped the smoothie. "You know I've identified the usher. Probably. We haven't found Michael Stevens yet through DM V." "We winnowed through the bunch of them and found his address. We haven't tracked him down yet."

"How hard is that?"

"He hasn't been home. His neighbors don't know when he'll be back. It takes information to generate leads."

"That's the oldest excuse in the book." She shook her now empty onion ring bag and stole one of Caleb's. "I talked to Dr. Bartholomew, one of her professors. Renee's adviser, Marcy Irvine, is out of the country."

"Yep. Talked to the professor, too," Caleb said. "And we talked to the man who funded Renee's fellowship today. There's something there, but I don't think he killed her. We'll check his alibi all the same."

"Caleb, she was beautiful. She surrounded herself with men. It doesn't take much to imagine their relationship." "Not everyone is like that."

Dani stared at him. "That's exactly what our relationship was."

"Only because I pushed. I'm sorry, Dani. That was the worst mistake of my life. If I could redo it, I would."

She stood so fast the stool fell to the ground. "I was a mistake?" Hot tears slipped from her eyes, and she swatted them away.

"That's not what I meant." Caleb groaned and hung his head. "I took what wasn't mine. You deserved better. When I went to college that fall, I hooked up with a couple guys on my dorm floor who were Christians, real Christians. After watching them a semester, I realized they had something I never did. A relationship with Christ that transformed how they acted. That's what I wanted. I came back that next summer and looked for you. But you'd disappeared."

"Do you have any idea what happened?" Sobs shook her. She

wrapped her arms around her stomach. "Caleb, I was pregnant. You left and never looked back. I had to make all the decisions. Alone. Sixteen. Nobody caring about me."

His face drained of color. He took a hesitant step toward her. "You never told me."

"My parents were so horrified, they swore they'd never let me come back. Dad wanted me to get an abortion, but I couldn't do that." Caleb took another step toward her, and Dani backed into the wall. She slid to the floor. "Aunt Jayne was the only one who supported me. The only one who cared." "But you knew where my family lived. Why didn't you call or let them know?" He eased down in front of her.

"You left me!" she screamed. "You took what you wanted and abandoned me to live with the consequences."

"What...what did you decide?"

"I placed the baby for adoption." Dani lowered her head to her knees and wept.

Caleb scooted next to her. "I am so sorry, Dani. I had no idea." She looked up to find tears trailing down his face. "If I'd known..."

"Nothing would have changed. Would you have married me? What choice did we have? We were two kids."

He pushed a clump of hair from her face. "Was it a girl or a boy?"

Dani hiccuped and swallowed hard. Images of holding the baby, knowing what she had to do, flooded her. She'd wanted to keep her daughter, but knew she couldn't, not without her parents' support. Not without Caleb. She couldn't fight them alone. "She was beautiful, Caleb. So perfect." A shudder coursed through her, and she swiped her cheeks. "She had this head of dark hair and precious rosebud lips. She was all pink and wrinkly, but incredible. The best thing I did was give her to her adoptive parents, but it broke my heart."

Caleb pulled her into a careful embrace, and she wept the tears she'd stored since that day. "Do you get photos? Updates?" "It was a closed adoption. I left a letter with the agency in case she ever wants to find me."

Caleb winced at her words. He gently rocked her as the sobs

eased. "I don't know what to say. I should have never pushed you. And I should have been there for you."

Dani nodded. "It was horrible. But I did what I had to." She should ease away from his embrace, but she couldn't. So many nights she'd lain in bed and wished Caleb knew. She laid her head on his shoulder.

"What do we do now?" Caleb stroked her hair.

"Find a killer?"

"No, Dani. What about us? Will you give me another chance?"

Could she do that? Could she trust him after everything that had happened? "I don't know. It couldn't be like last time, Caleb."

He turned her toward him and looked into her eyes. His eyes were darker than usual, tinged with sincerity. "I want it to be different. Let me treat you like the treasure you are. I want to protect you, Dani. Love you without strings or demands."

As she stared into his eyes, Dani held tight to her anger. Yes, he'd cried. He'd even apologized. But it wasn't enough. Too much time had passed, and she still hurt too much from giving up her baby. Their baby. Job trotted into the room and pushed his way between them with a snort. Dani rubbed behind his ears. "I can't, Caleb."

His shoulders sagged and he opened his mouth as if to argue, then stopped. The Caleb she'd interacted with this week seemed very different from the self-centered college- bound student she'd known. But it was too soon to know if he was sincere.

Maybe they could reclaim what they'd lost? Make the lost years disappear? She shook her head. That was way too risky. She pushed away from Caleb and started to clean up the dishes.

Job headbutted Caleb, who rubbed Job's ears. Even after her refusal, he didn't seem in a hurry to leave, and Job certainly enjoyed the attention. Dani finished cleaning and glanced at the clock.

"Don't you need to go home or back to the station?"

"Not tonight. I thought I'd sleep on the couch, make sure you were okay."

The thought made Dani stiffen. Had his words been so cheap that ten minutes after telling her he wanted a new kind of relationship, he thought he could camp out?

He stood and leaned against the counter. "Dani, I don't mean what you think. I just want to make sure nothing happens here."

"I'll be okay. There's nothing to indicate he'll hurt me."

"Other than the fact this person knows where you live?"

"I promise I won't let anyone in and will lock the doors. I'll even let you take me to work, since you commandeered my car."

"We'll have it back to you as soon as it's processed." "Please, Caleb. You can't stay. I'll call if anything happens. Promise."

He studied her as if measuring her resolve. "All right. Isn't there anyone I can call or that you can stay with?"

"Nope." She shrugged. "You're really the only person I know outside of work. It's too late to bother Aunt Jayne or Tricia anyway." She shooed Caleb toward the door.

"I'll leave, Dani, but I'll watch from outside. Be careful." He leaned down, and she stiffened. He lightly kissed her on the cheek and pushed a strand of hair behind her ear. "See you soon."

She closed and locked the door behind him. The night had gone nothing like she'd planned. What would Caleb do when he processed what she'd told him. "Come on, Job, let's get to bed." Job trotted beside her, nose to her knee, as she went upstairs. Together they entered her bedroom, and Dani got ready for bed. Pulling the covers to her chin, she felt empty. She longed for her daughter to be tucked next to her, even as she knew a ten-year-old wouldn't want to cuddle with her mom. If only she could turn back the clock. Change her decisions, starting with dating Caleb. She hoped she wouldn't regret telling him her story or allowing him back into her life. Her eyes drifted shut as she settled in under the covers...

Dani runs down a narrow alley. Buildings tower on either side. Their top stories practically touch and scrape the starless night sky. She opens her mouth, desperate to pull another gasp of air to her emptying lungs. Her chest pounds, ready to explode. She struggles to keep running, to get away from her shadowy pursuer. Her feet sink into the cement. She slogs through quicksand, and each step pulls her deeper into the mire.

With each step she falls farther behind. Somewhere in the inky blackness, he chases her.

She feels him close in, imagines his breath hot on her neck.

She can't see his face.

Why do you pursue me? All she knows is in another block he 'll catch her.

Frantically, Dani searches every corner and crevice for an escape. She needs a door; a corner where she can hide. She sees none. It is hopeless.

In the distance, a siren squeals. Even it can't help her. Running is meaningless, a futile attempt to avoid the inevitable.

Dani's eyes popped open, her chest heaving as she struggled to release the shadowy dream. Her pajamas clung to her body, soaked in sweat.

A shrill noise pierced the darkness. What time was it? She searched the surface of her nightstand, feeling for her clock: 3:30 a.m. No wonder she was exhausted. She groped for the phone. No, that was a book. A stack of magazines. A glass of water.

Another ring sliced the darkness. Dani jumped and magazines slithered off the table. *Where was the phone?* There. Dani felt its plastic contours. She squinted as she flipped on the table lamp. *Please don't let this be the stalker.* She punched the talk button. "Hello?" she croaked.

"Did you like your tires? Consider it a gift." The disembodied voice laughed.

With a jolt, Dani's fingers released the phone and it fell. She groped the carpet at the side of her bed for it. With a grimace, she held the phone to her ear. Nothing but a buzz.

16

While the murderer enjoyed freedom, the precinct had formed prison bars around Caleb. Trapping him with a case that refused to move forward. He scanned Denimore and Westmont's reports from the previous day, but nothing groundbreaking appeared on the paper. Nothing had been called in overnight, either. The weight of the investigation pushed him into a slump at the conference table.

He needed answers. So did Renee's family. Her parents would arrive later in the morning, hoping for answers he couldn't provide. It'd taken Westmont a couple days to find them. Their reaction at the news had been total silence. Caleb wanted to be able to give them the news that the police had caught the murderer. At this point, that looked highly unlikely.

Her parents would fly into town and leave with the body if the coroner released it. With a start, he refocused on this paper. Anything to create distance from his memories, which refused to recede. Bowing his head, words flowed through his mind. *Father, I'm at a loss. Lead me. Bring justice to this situation. You are a just God, and I need justice. Renee Thomas's family needs justice. Use me as an instrument.*

Guide me and the team as we seek answers. I am so grateful You already know them.

Sometimes peace descended after prayer. This morning, he stared at the whiteboard covered with chicken scratch notes and waited. *I know nothing's a surprise to You, Lord. Even when life is anything but predictable here.*

"Hey, boss." Westmont threw a waxy white bag on the table in front of Caleb. "Your favorite, a bear claw. What do you have for us?"

Caleb opened the bag and smiled at the scent of cinnamon and icing. Fortification for the day. He took a bite followed by a quick swig of coffee. Time to pick up Dani. He grabbed the printout of Michael Stevens's driver's license record and headed for his car.

AS THE SUN painted warm colors across the morning sky, Dani felt invigorated after her jog. She brushed on the last touches of makeup, then slipped a blazer over her red silk blouse. Downstairs she filled Job's food and water bowls. The dog's tongue still hung out of his mouth after their race around the neighborhood. He'd pulled her the whole way then collapsed in the kitchen.

She locked the door behind her, making sure the dead bolt had slipped into place. For a moment she looked fruitlessly for her red Mustang, before noticing the dark-haired man and his nondescript sedan. She walked toward Caleb with a smile.

"Good morning." Caleb's face was tight and shadowed. It looked like he'd thought about her revelation. A lot.

"Morning." Dani stopped a few feet in front of him and crossed her arms. He wouldn't ask her to start over today. "When will my car be released?"

"Not sure yet, but if it's not today, you can get a rental car."

He helped her into the car, then handed her a folder. "Here's a copy of Michael Stevens's driver's license. Is this your usher?" Dani studied the sheet, memorizing the address. "It looks like him, though it's hard to tell with the grainy picture." "We'll keep looking for him then. And, Dani?"

"Yes?"

"Don't go looking for him on your own."

"Yes, sir." Nope, she'd just take Logan with her.

Caleb dropped her off at Channel 17. Dani hopped from the car, relieved to escape the tension. She was an hour early. Plenty of time to review the tape of last night's newscast. See what she'd missed. She took the tape to edit bay 3, turned on the monitor and tape deck and popped in the tape. The screen blinked to life, and she scanned to segment two of the newscast. She slowed the tape as the prior story ended, and Phil appeared on the screen.

His voice slowed and his expression added just the right touch of sadness to his usual calm presence.

He hit the appropriate emotions like the pro he was. She listened as the story continued. After the last sound bite,

Phil came back on. He looked into the camera, fumbling with

√

the papers.

That wasn't his usual style. Why would Phil react to this story? But then, why had he stopped by the scene on Thursday? Dani headed back to her desk, questions whirling through her mind. He had acted a little off all week. She entered Phil's name in a search engine. The first link led to an article about a celebrity gala fundraiser.

Hands landed on either side of her chair back. Dani jumped and tried to turn the chair around, but someone held it in place. Craning her neck, she met Phil's glare. "You scared me to death. What are you doing?"

"Just reading over your shoulder. I love to read my press. Looking for something?"

"Learning more about the stars I work with. I use Google to find information about all of you." She shot him a smile tinged with coquettishness as Phil examined her.

With a smirk, he pushed her chair into the desk before he

released his hold and turned out of the cube. The scent of his musky cologne lingered. Dani waved her hand to clear the air, and then turned back to the monitor. She clicked back to the search page and hit the second entry.

Dani looked up Tricia Jamison's number and dialed it. She couldn't investigate Phil inside the studio. Maybe Tricia would help. They'd been friends before everything fell apart with Caleb. "Hi, Tricia. Could you meet me at Joe's Place this morning? Really? Fifteen minutes would be great. Thanks."

Dani grabbed keys to the station's little Neon, and took off for Joe's. Ten minutes later, Dani pushed open the heavy door to the cafe as a bell announced her presence. She ordered her standard mocha cappuccino and grabbed a table for two. Soothing jazz piped through the coffee shop's sound system. Dani tapped along to the beat and waited for Tricia.

When the bell chimed Tricia's approach, Dani waved and straightened her jacket. Tricia must spend a fortune on designer suits. A warm smile creased Tricia's face.

"It's so good to see you, Dani. Your call was well timed. I'd just finished a quick conference at court." She slipped out of her jacket and placed it on the back of her chair. "Let me grab a coffee and I'll be right back."

How could Tricia help? What could she really hope to accomplish?

"Okay. Fill me in. If this is about the murder, I'm happy to help. Caleb won't go home until the case is solved. As if a case will fall apart if he gets a decent night's sleep. Men." She rolled her eyes and smiled. "What do you need?"

"Can you apply attorney-client privilege to this?" The last thing Dani needed was Phil finding out she had an attorney investigating him.

"Give me a dollar, and you're my client for purposes of research and investigation."

Dani rummaged through her billfold, pulled out a dollar and slid it across the table. "Can you do a background check on Phil Baker? I don't know what I expect, but he's hiding something."

"I'll have to think about how best to do that." Tricia frowned and tapped a manicured finger against the tabletop. "The firm frowns on employees using its resources for personal reasons. Plus he's well known. It'll be hard to keep it secret. But I'll see what I can do. Anything else?"

"I don't know." Dani twisted a strand of hair before tucking it behind her ear. "This whole investigation has been strange. Someone slashed my tires last night. One wasn't enough, so they slashed all four."

"Be careful, okay." Tricia glanced at her watch. "I've got to run back to court."

"Thanks for meeting me." Dani pulled a card out of her purse and wrote her cell number on it. "You can call me on my cell anytime. Thanks for your help, Tricia."

"No problem. I'm glad you called. It's been too long." Tricia pushed back from the table and stood. "I'll call when I know something."

"Thanks." Dani watched Tricia leave, hoping she'd have some information for her later today. Now for the hard call.

Somehow she had to talk Caleb into letting her into Renee's house. With a bit of fast talking, she got him to agree to meet her there. She called Logan on the way. "Meet me at Renee Thomas's house. I'm trying to talk our way in."

Logan whistled, and Dani yanked her cell away from her ear. "Good luck with that."

"Just get there, okay?"

She pulled the Neon onto O Street and headed north toward Thirty-third. From there she'd find Renee's home without problem. Dani followed Thirty-third to the neighborhood. Large trees overshadowed the stately residences, casting a soothing peace over the wide streets. She tried to keep her eyes focused on the road when all she wanted to do was soak in the beauty of the stone and brick architecture.

As she parked her car in front of the house, Dani didn't see Logan's Jeep on the cul-de-sac. She approached the house. Closed curtains prevented her from peeking through the windows on either side of the front door. Dani slid her sunglasses to the top of her head and started around the side of the house. The lawn stood an inch or two taller than the neighbors' and a few scraggly bushes and perennials dotted the side lawn.

She waited on the front step for the guys. If she couldn't talk Caleb into letting them in, maybe Logan's friendship would do it.

Logan approached with a matching grin, while Caleb looked less than happy to be there.

"What do you need, Dani? Want a look around the house?" "Yes. That's exactly what I want."

"I can't. It hasn't been released yet. I'm sorry, but you have to be content with the outside."

"Could you at least part the curtains?" Dani pulled her sunglasses through her hair and lowered them to shield her eyes.

"Then you'd want to see the foyer, and next thing I'd be talking to the captain about how a sealed house was invaded by the media. Sorry, Dani."

"We can still use the house as the backdrop for your live shot for the noon show." Logan walked to the Jeep and pulled out a camera and tripod.

Dani turned and looked at the house. "What is it about this place? It feels like a piece of the puzzle, but why?"

Caleb settled on the step. "It is. Off the record?" She nodded. "Phil Baker sold this house to Renee Thomas two months before her death."

"That might explain the sterile appearance."

"I knew you saw more than you let on."

Dani shrugged. "But I still need more."

"You and the rest of the media." He swiped his hand across shadowed eyes. He reached over, then hesitated before brushing a strand of hair from Dani's face. She stilled, avoiding his eyes. "We're doing everything we can to figure out what's going on. But you have to be careful. Phil sold her the house for next to nothing, and we're trying to figure out why." Fatigue settled on Dani, making it difficult to form a coherent thought. "I'm so tired."

She longed to lean into him, take comfort from his quiet strength. "Every time I turn around, I find another message on my answering machine. I don't know what to do." She rubbed her forehead, trying to ease the headache that radiated pain.

"You'll get through this. Just don't investigate on your own. I can't keep an eye on you when you do that." He stood and headed to his car. "I've got a meeting with a family this afternoon and an investigation to finish."

Dani looked across the cul-de-sac and noticed people working in their yards. Folks who hadn't been home Saturday. "Grab that camera, Logan. Let's interview some more neighbors."

17

As soon as Dani crossed the street trailed by Logan, the neighbors congregated on the sidewalk. A couple of moms had babies and toddlers harnessed in strollers. A middle-aged woman wearing a large straw hat peeled off her gardening gloves and approached Dani. Laugh lines deepened around her brown eyes as she approached.

"Young lady, do you know what happened to that poor girl?"

"No, but we're trying to find out. Did any of you know her?" The gardener shook her head. "She kept to herself."

"She didn't live here long." The young mom pulled a pacifier from beside her baby in the stroller. She stuck it in the wailing infant's mouth. "Two, three months at most."

"Did she live by herself?"

"Yes, but a man was there a lot. Always coming and going at the strangest times of the day." The gardener brandished her gloves through the air. "You know kids these days. No longterm commitment."

Dani cringed at the commentary as she took notes. Had the woman seen Phil or Reed Donovan?

The young mom rolled her eyes. "Yes, Gladys. Let's lump them all into one immoral lump. Renee never had loud parties and only had one guy over at a time. She didn't disturb us. It's hard to imagine why someone would kill her."

"I agree. She seemed very likeable the time I met her." Dani looked at her notepad. "Can you tell me anything about those you saw going into her home?"

Gladys harrumphed. "The one was distinguished looking and older. Made me think of one of the local anchors every time I saw him."

"The other was more bookish."

"Wait. Which anchor?" Dani tried to hide her excitement. Maybe Phil hadn't just sold Renee the house.

"Oh, they all look alike to me. Dark hair. Guy next door, all-American."

The mom shook her head. "I'd say he was younger than most, maybe late thirties."

In a small market like Lincoln, late thirties was actually old. Most anchors and reporters started their careers here and were only a few years out of college. These descriptions didn't limit the pool of possibilities.

"Anything else?" She smiled as the women talked over each other to give trivia about Renee. "Logan, grab their names while I get ready for the newscast."

While Dani had interviewed the neighbors, the live truck had pulled into the cul-de-sac. Tom Young, the truck operator, had it set up with antennae pointed toward the sky and clear of electrical lines.

"Need anything from me, Tom?"

"Not yet. We'll be ready for the air in thirty minutes." "Perfect. I'll put the story together." Dani wandered back to the stairs and sat down.

"Yoo-hoo, Dani." Doris waved from her yard. "I've got some tea and cookies for you."

"Thank you. Did you make them yourself?"

"Oh yes. Fresh this morning. Thought you looked like you could use the sustenance." Doris headed toward the door. "Come over here. I'll only be a second."

Dani settled onto the stoop and grinned when Doris appeared with a plate loaded with cookies. "I love snickerdoodles. My Aunt Jayne always made them for me. I tried once but forgot the cream of tartar."

Doris wrinkled her nose. "They wouldn't be very good without it."

"Trust me, they were awful." Dani took a bite and savored the buttery treats.

"So what do you think of my neighbors?"

"Nice women."

"You didn't spend enough time around Gladys then. She's got quite a tongue on her."

They chatted for several minutes while Dani enjoyed the cookies and mint tea.

"I'll let you get back to work, dear."

"Thanks for the snack."

"My pleasure." Doris hurried back to her yard, waving before she slipped into her house.

Dani stood, crumbs falling from her suit.

"It's time, Dani." Tom stood outside the truck holding a lapel mic. "You're on in ten minutes. Logan's got your b-roll put together and needs to know which bites you want to use."

No rest for the weary.

After the live report, Dani waved at the group of women who had crossed the street to watch her report. She felt like a celebrity for a minute as they oohed and aahed over her poise.

Dani headed to the Neon ready to grab a bite to eat and resume the hunt for Reed Donovan, Renee's boyfriend. Her cell phone rang and she grabbed it. "Hello?"

"Hey, Dani. This is Tricia. It's been a crazy day, but I'm working on Baker's background check. I had a thought, though. What about Renee's family? I don't think I've heard anything about them."

Dani grabbed her briefcase from the car. "We haven't had any luck tracking them down."

"I didn't have time to do much, but it looks like they're from a Chicago suburb. I called their number. If it's the right one, they aren't home."

"Thanks, Tricia. I'll run with that."

Popping open the briefcase on the hood, she sorted through the notepads she'd brought with her, throwing the useless ones in the footwell. "It has to be here somewhere."

"What has to be there?"

Dani banged her head against the doorframe as she turned to see Logan standing behind her, tripod in one hand, equipment bag thrown over the other shoulder. She rubbed the tender spot on her head. "Quit sneaking up on me."

"I wasn't sneaking, you're just absorbed. What has you muttering?"

Dani glared at him, then turned back to the stack of notepads. "You know we haven't been able to locate Renee's parents. Where's a logical place to find them?"

"At their house?"

"But they've never answered their phone. They'll come here. Renee's body hasn't been released yet." A spark of hope ignited in Dani. They're on their way here. Who better to confirm Renee was involved with Phil or whoever than a mom or sister she tells all her secrets to? "We have to find them, Logan."

Logan pulled off his station baseball cap and rubbed his forehead. "Didn't Caleb say something about a family to deal with?"

"Yes. What do you bet it's Renee's parents?" She opened her cell phone and pulled up Caleb's number. "Hey, Caleb. Are you with Renee Thomas's parents?" A thrill shot through her. "Could you ask if they'd talk to me on or off camera? On is preferable."

She waited, tapping her toes as muffled sounds of Caleb talking filtered to her. "Thank you! Where can we meet them?" Tucking the phone against her shoulder, Dani scribbled down directions. "See you then."

She closed the phone and climbed into the car. "They'll meet us at the airport before their flight leaves."

"All right. When?"

Logan closed the Jeep's hatch. "Caleb said he'd have them there in an hour and a half."

Grieving parents. Dani could understand a shadow of what they felt. She wished she had more than compassion to offer.

Was there something she could beseech for help? "God, it would be nice if You existed like Aunt Jayne and others believe. I need help." She must be stressed. She couldn't deny the part of her that wanted the peace and security she'd seen in Aunt Jayne, Logan, and even Caleb. Once upon a time she'd thought she had it, too, but that was before she had to give up her daughter.

The airport complex came into view with the National Guard post to the south. Dani followed Logan into the ground parking lot and to the terminal.

"Where are we meeting them?"

"The little bar on the second floor. They won't arrive for a while."

While Logan set up, Dani wandered the wide hallway. She kept an eye on the escalator for Caleb and the Thomases. The minutes crawled by until a dark head caught her attention. A couple trailed Caleb. He whisked them past her into the restaurant. Dani started to follow, but he stopped her.

"Give us a minute, Dani." Soon, he returned for her. "They're ready now."

"Did you tell them I found Renee?"

"That's why they'll talk with you. Come on."

A couple huddled together at a corner table in the restaurant, shoulders turned inward and away from the door.

Dani looked from the couple to Caleb. "Are they ready to talk to me?"

"I don't think 'ready' is the right word, but I'll introduce you.

Don't push them. They just left the morgue an hour ago. The medical examiner won't release the body, so they're going home empty hand- ed." Caleb's tone softened.

"I'll be gentle. I only have a few questions." She walked past him and approached the table. "Mr. and Mrs. Thomas? I'm Dani Richards. I'm so sorry about Renee."

The couple were in their fifties. Gray laced Mrs. Thomas's hair and grief shrouded her eyes. Mr. Thomas placed a protective arm around her shoulder and pulled her closer. His brown eyes searched Dani's and then returned to his wife. "Please have a seat, Miss Richards. I'm Jason Thomas. This is my wife Rebecca."

"I met Renee twice. I interviewed her for a story on her research. She was so excited about it that I wanted to understand more. Then I saw her again at the theater the night she was killed."

Mr. and Mrs. Thomas looked at each other. Mrs. Thomas's chin quivered as she turned toward Dani. "When you saw my daughter at the theater, was anyone with her?"

"No, but I think she expected someone. Renee looked striking in a beautiful emerald dress and had her hair swirled in a chignon. And in the moments we talked I remember wishing I had her poise."

"Her father and I worked hard to give her every advantage. We even sent her to finishing school. Then she came here for graduate school. Everything fell apart."

"How?"

"She'd always excelled in school with a bent for math and science. We hoped she'd choose medical school, but she decided to do this food thing instead. Then she bought a house here. She asked us for a little money to help, but we could only manage a few thou- sand. I didn't want her to settle here." A sob interrupted her words, and Mr. Thomas folded his tall frame so he could rub her knee while continuing to hold her. She brought a Kleenex to her face and shud- dered. "How did this happen?"

"Did she talk about friends or boyfriends when she called home?"

"Renee seemed to attract men without effort, but school filled her world." Mrs. Thomas looked from her husband to her hands. Mr. Thomas edged closer to her, and she seemed to gather herself. "What aren't the police telling us? Investigator Jamison asked similar questions."

Dani hesitated as she felt Caleb's stare from the next table. Part of their grief settled on her. She knew with everything in her they deserved any answers she could offer. Her gaze met Caleb's, and she pleaded silently to tell them something. He nodded once with warning in his eyes. She'd have to be careful, but the Thomases needed what little she knew.

"Mrs. Thomas, I'd be lying if I told you we know what happened to Renee." Dani reached for the woman's free hand and held it lightly. "We don't know why she was killed or who did it. The police have worked round the clock on that problem, and I've worked on my own. I don't know why I found your daughter, but I take that responsibility seriously. I will do everything I can to find her killer."

Dani took a breath and pushed forward. "Something led to Thursday night. Do you have any idea who Renee expected to join her? The murder was close and intimate. That suggests a boyfriend."

Mr. Thomas hugged his wife closer to his chest. "Miss Richards, we appreciate what you're saying but that's not our Renee. All she talked about was school. We don't know if she had friends, let alone boyfriends."

Mrs. Thomas placed a finger on his lips, stopping her husband's flow of words. "Honey, she was excited after meeting that reporter at a football game. Sounded like an excited teenager." Mrs. Thomas looked at Dani. "But she never mentioned him again. Then she called about the theater last week. Her voice vibrated with excitement, but she was coy about who was taking her. We got interrupted, and she said she'd fill me in afterwards."

Dani fought tears as Mrs. Thomas broke into fresh sobs. Caleb placed his hand on her shoulder as he cleared his throat. "Mr. and Mrs. Thomas, we should get you to your gate."

"I'm so sorry for your loss. Thank you for your time." Dani eased from the table and walked toward the table where Logan waited. She wished she possessed a silver tongue that spoke the right words at moments like this. Instead, her words had made the grieving couple cry. She sat in the chair next to his and watched the couple gather their bags. "They deserve answers about what happened to Renee, and I'm going to find them."

18

The station buzzed with activity as Caleb shuffled to the conference room. Guys shouted greetings he barely heard. His thoughts were caught in a twisted pile. Walking Renee Thomas's parents through the coroner's office had brought a heaviness to his steps. Images of identifying his father's battered body were superimposed over Renee Thomas and her parents. He'd fought dry heaves just like that day.

Then the image of a little girl dressed all in pink pirouetted through his mind. Tears clouded his vision at the reality of all he had lost. His heart ached at the loss. Why? He hadn't even known he had a daughter until hours earlier. A burning replaced the ache at the thought of what he'd been denied.

"You look terrible, Jamison." Westmont crossed his arms and stared at Caleb.

"Thanks. I could say the same of you." Caleb ran a hand over his head. "While I dealt with grieving parents, what did you learn?"

"I've scoured the victim's bank account until I can hardly see straight. All the numbers are swimming across the page."

Caleb spun a finger in the air, and Westmont caught the hint.

"She didn't have extra income. A small stipend from mom and dad. Her TA money from the university. That's it. Looks like she spent it in the standard places, too. Denimore's checking on a rental car transaction she had a few weeks ago. She also took a trip to Chicago a month ago."

Caleb felt a pulse of excitement.

"Her folks didn't mention a visit." Caleb plopped in a chair and scanned the record. It contained barebones information. "Follow up on that. Her mom insisted they hadn't seen Renee since Christmas."

"I wondered about that. Why go home and not see them?" "Exactly." Caleb flipped a page. "What about this debit charge at Oxford's? That's a pricey men's shop. An interesting choice for a single woman. Do we have a receipt?" "Haven't seen one, but I'll call the shop."

"The listing says cologne. I want to know what kind, and if Baker wears it. Let's get Baker's accounts."

"DA insists we don't have enough to get a warrant yet." "That's the story of this investigation."

Westmont flipped a sheet of paper in his notepad. "We found Stevens. He's working over at Valentino's on O Street. We'll pay him a visit when his shift ends."

Caleb smiled for the first time in hours. Maybe they were getting somewhere.

DANI PULLED into a parking spot on campus. She'd called Reed Donovan, and he'd promised to stay in his office until she got there. She entered the chemical engineering building and proceeded to room 412. The door was shut, and she groaned. "Don't do this."

Didn't he know that if he ran, he'd look guilty?

Dani tried the knob, but the door was locked. She walked down the hallway and stepped into the first open office. "Sony to bother you, but have you seen Reed Donovan? We had an appointment."

The man looked over his bifocals at her. "No. He teaches a class earlier in the afternoon, and usually leaves after that." "Thanks." Dani circled the floor, but didn't find anyone else who had seen Reed. Her phone rang, and she answered it as she walked to the Neon. "Dani Richards."

"Where are you? Kate's about ready to blow her top." "I'm on campus. Reed Donovan ignored our appointment. I'll be there in five minutes to put the packages together." Her packages highlighted Renee's parents and their grief. In St. Louis, the murder would have dropped from the newscast after the weekend. Since violent crime was rarer in Lincoln, she could develop the story.

She watched the five-thirty package with Logan. "I hope this story finally generates something for the police."

"It can't hurt. Need a ride home?"

"No, Kate told me to use the Neon as long as I need." Dani grimaced. "It's definitely not my Mustang. I think she's afraid I'll sue the station."

"Over slashed tires?"

"Crazier things happen." Dani shrugged. She looked for any reason to stay. Home seemed like a place to avoid, but she didn't have anywhere else to go.

THE CONFERENCE ROOM was empty for the moment. The silence mocked Caleb. The credits for the five-thirty newscast played on the TV in the corner. Dani would head home soon. He hated the idea of Dani home alone, but couldn't stomach the thought of seeing her. She wasn't taking the notes and slashed tires seriously enough. And she'd dug her heels in when he pressed, refusing to back down. Why couldn't she have been this stubborn ten years ago? Since her confession last night, thoughts of that summer so long ago and his sin wouldn't leave him. He'd been selfish, focused only on college and what he wanted. That guilt vied with his anger, each taking a turn dominating his thoughts.

He clenched his teeth as pain nearly doubled him over. What had he done? *God, why did You let her go through that? Why let me find out now?* He'd never be able to understand this. How could God work this out for good? That summer Dani had become so close to God. She'd fairly glowed with joy. Now she seemed lost.

She'd known about their daughter. If hot shards of pain pierced him at the thought that he had a little girl, he could only imagine what she'd experienced. She'd held her. Kissed her. Released her. And kept her from him. They could have been a family. Instead, he'd never get to know his own flesh and blood.

After staring at a file but seeing only a little girl, he threw it to the table and stormed out of the conference room. He might not be able to do anything about his daughter, but he'd make sure Dani was okay, push past the distraction. Prove to himself anything he felt for her was dead.

He was waiting on Dani's back step, when she pulled into her parking spot.

An uneasy smile creased her face when she spotted him. "Hi."

"Hey." He stood and walked down the stairs toward her. "Had supper yet?" He watched her, unsure what he wanted her to answer and why he'd asked.

She shook her head.

"How about Valentino's?" The name tripped off his tongue. He'd been hungry for good pizza all day. And it used to be her favorite. He wondered if it still was.

"Isn't that where Michael Stevens works?"

"He's not at the location we'll use."

"I wasn't looking forward to an evening alone."

An uneasy silence fell as they entered the kitchen, and Job bounded outside. In a minute he scratched to come back in. The dog shadowed her every move. Caleb half expected Job to get tangled around her ankles. Great. Then he could save her from the dog he made her get.

Dani ordered a large pizza. Hungry as he was, it might not be enough. Thirty minutes later, the doorbell rang, and Caleb could almost taste his first bite. Nobody made pizza on a crust as good as Valentino's.

"I've got it." He opened the door.

The deliveryman started at the motion, then thrust the pizza at his chest.

"A gift for Miss Richards."

Before Caleb could react, the man ran back down the stairs. Caleb threw the box on the entry table and hurried after him. By the time he rounded the corner, a small hatchback with a Valentino's sign strapped to the top was disappearing into the darkness. Caleb tried to decipher the license plate number in the gloom, but couldn't. He headed back to Dani's and went inside.

"Was that the delivery guy?" Dani's voice echoed down the hallway.

Caleb looked at the pizza in his hand. "You could say that." He searched the darkness another minute before closing the door and taking the pizza to the kitchen. "Dani, Michael Stevens delivered the pizza. A gift for you. He threw the box at me and ran."

Dani stilled, frozen in place where she stretched to reach a glass stashed in the cupboard. She forced her body to respond to the everyday commands her brain had forwarded. "What did you say? Free?"

"He left before I could pay or grab him." Caleb tossed the box on the island. As he repeated the words, she sagged against the counter.

"Is there a note on the box?"

"No. It looks clean. I'm sorry, Dani."

"How did he know I ordered a pizza?"

"I don't know, since he works at Valentino's across town. Maybe he's filling in?" Caleb lifted the pizza lid.

Dani inhaled the aroma of spiced tomato and pepperoni that wafted in the air. Her stomach rebelled at the thought of eating it. "Give me that. There's no way we can eat it now." She threw the box on the back steps. "What can I get you to drink? I'll make spaghetti."

She filled glasses with soda, her mind racing. Had she misread Michael Stevens? Maybe he really was a pizza deliveryman. If that was it, wouldn't he want to be paid? Nothing made sense anymore. "Aunt Jayne treated me to Valentino's during my visits growing up. Some things never change." She filled a pot with water, keeping her back to Caleb.

"Dani." Caleb's tone warned she couldn't avoid him.

She slid spaghetti into the boiling water. Watched the water bubble. "I don't know what to do, Caleb. There's another message on the machine. Michael Stevens shows up at my house. My car is in custody. I'm looking over my shoulder. Jumping at strange sounds. What do you want me to do?" "Until I get a better handle on Stevens, I'll feel better if you don't spend the night alone." Job put his head in Caleb's lap, and he scratched the dog behind the ears. "Pack a bag. I'll take you to Tricia's for the night. Logan or I will feed and let Job out in the morning. You'll get a good night's sleep at Tricia's, and Job'll protect the house while you're away."

Dani shook her head and turned toward him. "No, Caleb. I'm not letting him push me around."

"You just finished saying you don't feel safe here." "That's not what I said. I won't let you twist my words." Caleb threw his hands in the air. "Do you think I want to be here right now? After last night's revelation?"

"So leave." She crossed her arms. "I'm not going to follow your instructions just because you feel guilty about something that happened ten years ago."

"You don't have any idea what I'm thinking." He pushed open the back door. "I need some air."

Dani watched him leave, torn between following him and storming to her room. The blink of the answering machine caught her attention. Much as she didn't want to admit it, Caleb was right. She shouldn't stay here.

The phone rang. Dani jumped, and then grabbed it. "Hello?" "Hey, Dani. It's Tricia. How would you like a gals' night out at my house?"

"Caleb told you to call." The guy couldn't quit, no matter how angry and hurt he was.

"Well...even if he did, that doesn't mean it wouldn't be fun. We need to catch up. And it's not like he'll be here." Tricia's voice softened. "You need a safe place for the night."

"There is that. Solve this murder, and that disappears." Dani turned off the burner under the spaghetti. "All right. I'll come. Give me about fifteen minutes."

Dani pulled together a bag for the night. A weight lifted from her as she locked her house. Then she saw her car. The Neon's windows were covered in red paint. The windshield sported a message: *Leave the investigation alone or the red won't be paint.* Dani stared at the car, and began to tremble. She searched the darkness, looking for anything. Tuned her ears for any out-of-place sound.

She unlocked the door and threw her bag inside. Like it or not, she needed Caleb. Again.

When he returned, Caleb took one look and pulled out his cell phone. "Your car was fine when I left."

"Let me guess. I just lost another car."

Caleb nodded. "We have to process it so we can build a case when we catch the guy."

"I'll wait in the house." She sat on the couch stroking Job behind the ears. *Find rest, O my soul, in God alone; my hope comes from Him. He alone is my rock and my salvation; He is my fortress, I will not be shaken... Pour out your heart to Him, for God is our refuge.* The words ran across her heart.

God, if you still care about me, would you be my refuge? Be my hope? My life is falling apart and I need a shelter. "Dani? The techs are here. Let me take you to Tricia's." "Let's go." Dani grabbed her bag and purse and headed for the door. After a short drive, they pulled up to a well cared for Cape Cod. It was everything Aunt Jayne's home could be with a little attention.

The front door bounced open, and Tricia rushed onto the porch. "Dani, are you okay? Caleb, grab her bag." Tricia ushered her into the house. "We'll give ourselves pedicures and watch a movie. I was thinking something sappy like *Princess Bride.*"

Dani grimaced. "I've never understood that movie."

"You never did? There's my movie collection, help yourself." Caleb cleared his throat and tossed Dani's bag on the couch. "I'll check in first thing in the morning. If you need anything, call. I'll have the phone beside me. You're safe here."

Dani nodded. She might be, if she could avoid *Princess Bride.*

19

Had Michael Stevens turned Dani's car into a tomato? Caleb stormed into the precinct, images of Dani's vehicle painted red pulsing through his mind. He slowed near dispatch. "Rikki, you seen Westmont?"

She shook her head, earrings jangling. "Nope. He's interviewing someone and hasn't checked back in."

Maybe it was Stevens. If so, the man had an alibi. Caleb tried to reach Westmont, but his phone kicked over to voice mail. He'd lie down until Westmont returned. Clear his head.

Caleb jerked awake when the overhead fluorescent light pierced his eyelids.

"Sorry, boss. Didn't know you were here." The grin on Westmont's face belied his words.

"There are kinder ways to wake me."

"They aren't as much fun."

"What time is it?"

"It's 7:00 a.m."

Caleb bolted upright. How had he slept that long?

"I've got a present for you." Westmont tossed a small bag at Caleb.

Caleb shook the bag. He tipped it over and a new toothbrush and razor slid out. "Always looking out for me."

"Somebody has to."

A few minutes later Caleb watched through the two-way mirror as an officer pushed Michael Stevens into a seat at the metal table in the interview room. Westmont had found him at his girlfriend's house. Stevens shot quick glances around the room... each time returning to the table in front of him. His heels tapped an erratic beat under the chair.

"Man's as nervous as a calf during branding season." Westmont stepped up to the mirror. "How you gonna approach him?"

"Slow and easy. Treat him like a friend." One that delivered free pizzas. "That'll knock him off balance since he's seen two hundred too many episodes of *Law and Order*." Caleb shook his head.

Stevens's twitches picked up tempo. His gaze flitted around the room.

"Showtime."

"Go get him."

Caleb opened the door and strode in. "Michael Stevens."

Stevens's head jerked up, and he shrunk into himself. "Y-yes?"

Caleb smiled at the discomfort the stutter revealed. Focus for twenty minutes, and he'd get the information he needed. *Give me the right words, Lord.*

"I'm Investigator Caleb Jamison. We met last night. I have a few questions we've asked other ushers who worked at the theater last Thursday night."

"Am I in trouble?" Stevens's features contorted into a mask.

"No. This shouldn't take too long. Why'd you leave the Lied before the police arrived Thursday night?"

"I got scared. What if the murderer stayed? I didn't want to be anywhere near that place." His gaze flicked around the room but didn't land anywhere.

Caleb pulled out a chair across from him and sat. "Why would the murderer stay?"

Stevens stiffened and turned away from him. "I can't say." "You won't get in trouble here unless you don't tell me everything you know about the murder." Stevens picked at nonexistent lint on his pullover sweater. "Why don't you tell me which section of the theater you worked that night."

"I worked the second floor. Helped guests find the right box or balcony entrance."

"Did you notice anything unusual?"

"Not during the rush of people finding their seats." Stevens wasn't making this easy. "What did you notice after the show started?"

Caleb tilted his chair back and waited for an answer. Stevens gulped. He looked at his hands where they twitched on the table. He launched from the table and dashed for the door. Westmont pushed Stevens back into his chair, then leaned against the door, blocking future escape attempts.

"Let's try again." Caleb leaned across the table into Stevens's space. "What's the story?"

"It's nothing."

"That's why you ran like a jackrabbit? Try again."

"A man came in shortly after that girl." Stevens stopped and looked from Caleb to Todd.

"Did he go into her box?"

"Yes."

"Do you know who it was?"

"Y-yes. Everybody in town knows him."

Adrenaline spiked through Caleb's body as he considered the best way to proceed. He could play 20 Questions with Stevens a long time. "What's his name?"

Stevens shook his head. "I can't say."

"Right. Let's play a game. I'll give you clues, and speak up when I'm close."

Stevens stared at the table.

"So, the man is prominent in the community."

"Yes."

"He works in the media."

"Y-yes. He's an anchor at Channel 17."

"When did Mr. Baker leave the box?"

"I don't know."

"You don't know? You'll have to try harder than that."

"I don't know. He gave me a twenty to get them some champagne. When I returned, the show had started, and I couldn't see anything. I left the champagne and didn't know anything was wrong until that gal yelled for help."

"You mean Dani Richards?"

Stevens nodded.

"Why corner her?"

"She works with him. Maybe they were in cahoots. Besides, she looked ready to bolt."

Caleb doubted that. He'd never seen her bolt from anything. "Why follow her to the parking garage later that night?"

"I didn't."

"She says you tried to stop her and hit her car as she left?"

"Sure she did." He leaned back.

"Why deliver a pizza to her house last night? Were you trying to scare her?" Caleb kept his face placid as Stevens blanched. "What? Think I wouldn't ask?"

"It's my job."

"To deliver a pizza and say it's a gift. Sure."

"I was filling in for a sick buddy. It's not even my usual location. I'll admit, it wasn't smart to throw it in your face." He threw his hands up, palm out, in front of him. "What were you doing at her house anyway? I wasn't expecting a cop."

"Maybe it was a good thing I was there."

Stevens snorted, as if the idea was ridiculous.

"How many times have you called her house?" Caleb leaned into his elbows on the table.

"I never have. I swear. Why would I call her?"

"We're done, but don't leave town. We might have more questions for you. Before you leave, Westmont will take your statement."

Caleb followed them out of the room. It wouldn't be long before he'd have probable cause and could finally get an arrest warrant for

Phil. Now, they could place Phil at the theater. It wasn't perfect, but they were a step closer. That was a marked improvement. He entered the conference room.

Running feet thundered outside the door. Caleb stuck his head out to see what was going on.

Stevens was sprawled outside the interview room. Westmont frantically compressed his chest. "Call an ambulance. Now!"

THE RICH SCENT of fresh coffee tickled Dani's nose and pulled her from sleep. She struggled to land back in the dream. Caleb had pulled her to him, sheltering her from someone. At a knock on the door, she pushed herself up and pulled the blue wedding ring quilt around her.

"Come in."

"Good morning. Did you get any sleep last night?" Tricia carried a tray loaded with two cups of coffee, a plate of muffins and a single yellow rose in a vase.

Dani made room on the bed for the tray. "For the first time in days, I did. Thanks for making that possible." She reached over to finger the delicate petals of the rose. "Where did this beauty come from?"

"A rosebush in my backyard." Tricia handed Dani a delicate teacup filled with coffee.

Dani watched Tricia over the top of the cup as she sipped the French vanilla brew. "This is the perfect wake up. Your house is peaceful."

"Remember going to church with Aunt Jayne?"

Dani shook her head trying to follow Tricia's conversation change. "Sure."

"Remember the story of Noah's Ark?"

"The animals walking two by two and tons of rain."

"That's the one. The Flood was the first storm, but not the last. Life is filled with them. For me it's clients or their crazy ex-husbands. For you at this moment, it's looking over your shoulder for the next threat." Tricia swirled her coffee. "Just like God had Noah build an ark to save his family, God provides an ark for the storms we live through. That's what this house is for me. It's a shelter in the storm."

"What about prayer and all those other things they always talked about?" The list of all the things she was supposed to do to get God to notice her filled Dani's thoughts.

"Those are important. You wouldn't believe how many times He gives me insight when I have a problem at work." A distant look settled into her eyes.

Dani mulled over Tricia's words. "Just talk to Him. You make it sound easy."

"It is." She propped her chin on her hands. "It's a conversation most days. But we have to ask Him for help. To save us and protect us from the storm. Then He can be our refuge."

Dani leaned against the headboard and struggled to follow Tricia. The only person she knew who talked like this was Aunt Jayne. As the last cobwebs of sleep cleared, peace and a shelter sounded so good. Even if it involved a God she couldn't see. "I've never heard Noah's Ark like that."

Tricia smiled at her and stood. "I have to be at court in an hour, so I need to run. Feel free to spend tonight here, too. I don't mind the company."

"Thanks. I'll see how today goes." And if she received any messages. She was tired of being afraid.

After Tricia left, Dani stayed in bed and fingered the velvety rose. The thin petals curled downward and orange tipped each petal. If God really had created everything like the Bible suggested, He'd done an amazing job with this flower.

Her phone trilled from the bedside table. "Time to face the day." Dani pushed back the quilt. Caleb's number flashed on the screen.

"Good morning."

Dani tucked a strand of hair behind her ear. "Tricia's a great hostess. Anything new?"

Caleb's sigh removed the last traces of peace from her morning. "We found Michael Stevens and interviewed him this morning."

She pulled the alarm clock over and stared at the time. "It's only eight-thirty, Caleb."

"I know. Todd brought him in before he disappeared again.

Good news is we talked to him. Bad news is he's in ICU right now."

"What did you do to him?"

"Just talked. No torture devices or anything. He keeled over after the interview."

"I guess I should feel safer now."

"Maybe, but we don't know he'd targeted you. Be careful around Phil."

Dani puffed a breath out. "Are you trying to keep me nervous?"

"Just watchful. Do you need a ride to the station this morning?"

"No. I've already scheduled a cab to take me to a rental agency. You're too busy to run me all over town." And she needed some distance from him.

"Call me if anything changes." She closed the phone. Time to move or she'd be late.

When she reached Channel 17, Logan followed her into the building.

"How's Job this morning?"

"He's fine, with the patience of his namesake."

Dani flopped into her chair. She pushed back and kicked her legs onto the desktop. "So?"

Logan grinned at her as he leaned against the cube's wall. "Just waiting for instructions."

She smirked at him. "You can get me some coffee. Two sugars and a dash of cream."

"Delighted, miss." He turned with a slight bow.

Dani sniffed as a heavenly scent filled the air. She turned and stilled. Tori held out a large bouquet of stargazer lilies.

"These arrived this morning."

"Thanks." Dani buried her nose in the bouquet, filling her lungs with the heady aroma. She pulled an envelope from the holder and opened it.

"Nice weeds." She looked up to see Logan standing there with two cups of coffee.

"No one's ever accused you of being romantic, have they?" After a moment, she pulled away from the lilies. "They're from my parents. Time to get to work." Now to locate Reed Donovan.

20

The newsroom buzzed with noise. She pulled her headphones out of the drawer and plugged in a jazz CD. Anything to help her focus. A saxophone wailed a soul rending melody, and she opened the Internet. Before she could type in the first search term, her phone rang.

"Richards."

Silence. Dani's stomach dropped as a sense of foreboding filled her. "Hello?"

"The clock is ticking." The words hissed into her ear, the voice, scrambled and unrecognizable. "Our game ends soon."

"What game?" Dani stood as she held the phone to her ear. She looked over the cubicle walls and scanned for Phil Baker. She could see a corner of his office across the maze of desks and walls. He sat at his computer, phone in the crook of his shoulder, nothing unusual. She sank into her chair, grabbed the armrest when she almost missed the seat.

"What do you want from me?" Her chest tightened as she said the words.

Laughter cackled in her ear. Then silence.

Dani dropped the phone as if it burned her fingers. Her hands trembled as she reached for a pen and wrote down garbled message. She rushed to the restroom and locked the door. Without a thought about her suit, she slid to the floor.

The doorknob twisted, followed by a bang on the door. "Hey, let us in."

Dani recognized the voice of Lynn Sailer, the overnight shift editor. She'd be a bear if Dani let her in. Instead, she let the minutes tick by until Lynn left, muttering about finding a key. Dani splashed cold water on her face. Looked in the mirror. The face that stared back at her looked haunted. Dark circles under her eyes had developed since Thursday. No amount of makeup could remove the evidence of her sleepless nights and worry filled thoughts.

Releasing the lock, Dani eased open the door. She headed for her desk and grabbed her purse.

"What are you doing?" Tori's words filled the space between them before Dani focused on her. "Your story's moved into the building. Get going."

"All right." Dani had no idea what Tori meant. She stepped past the producer into the newsroom.

Chaos filled the room. Officer Westmont strutted toward Phil's office. A couple of staffers fell into step behind him. Dani caught Logan's eye and waved him to the door.

She pushed around the clusters of conversation and picked up speed when she hit the door. "Grab your camera. The news came to us. They'll use the front doors."

Logan looked around the employee parking lot and nodded. "I'll meet you up front."

"This will go over like a lead balloon with Kate." The news director would react when the police led her star away in handcuffs. If that's why Officer Westmont was here.

Ten minutes later, Westmont walked out alone.

"I'll catch up in a minute, Logan." Dani walked across the clipped grass toward Officer Westmont's unmarked vehicle. "Officer, do you have a minute?"

"Hey, kid. What can I do for you?" He smiled at her and leaned against the open door as if he had all the time in the world.

Dani hesitated. Westmont shifted as he waited, but didn't rush her. "What were you doing here? I thought you planned to arrest Phil, and I doubt I'm the only one."

Westmont looked at her and then toward the door where Logan waited. "Off the record? We've placed him at the theater prior to the murder. That's all I can tell you. Jamison might have specifics." He considered her for a moment. "I just had a question till we can get enough to arrest him."

"And you enjoy rattling folks."

He grinned. "Known me a couple days and you've pegged me." He sobered. "Be careful, kid."

Dani followed Logan into the station. Her thoughts bounced between the phone message and Phil. She knocked on Kate Johansson's door. The news director sat at her desk gazing out the window behind her. At the knock, Kate swiveled to face her. "What do you need, Dani?"

"How do you want me to handle the story if Phil gets arrested? I plan to run with it since our competition will."

Kate nodded but looked past Dani at the pictures of local celebrities that lined her wall. "Treat it like any other story and him like any murder suspect."

"Did Westmont say anything to you?"

"No. Find out what you can and keep putting your stories together. If anything happens to Phil, I'll need to review the piece before you give it to the producers. Don't pull any punches." Kate's usual intense look replaced the distant one on her face. "Phil will have to live with the consequences of his actions. Get out there and cover the story."

Kate turned back toward the window in dismissal, and Dani slipped from the room. She joined Logan at the edit bay. "There's not enough for a story," he said.

"I know." She lowered her voice. "Before the police arrived at the station, I received a call with another message. Phil was on the phone at the same time, but the caller didn't sound like him." She shuddered at the memory of the strange laughter. "What if the police have the wrong man?"

"They'll figure it out."

"But will they figure it out before something happens to me?" "I've known Caleb a long time. Trust me, he'll get this right." Dani held her breath and hoped he was right. "Okay, let's go find Reed Donovan. He's teaching this morning. We'll wait outside his classroom."

"Sounds good. The Jeep's ready."

The search began when they arrived at the college. They wandered the chemical engineering building so long Dani wanted to throttle the next person who sent them in the wrong direction. Finally, she found Reed's classroom and slipped into the back. Reed Donovan tensed briefly when he noticed her, then settled back into his lecture in the half-empty lecture hall. His words flew over her head, so she took notes on the man.

Reed was tall and thin like Jimmy Stewart, but had a shock of red hair. He spoke in soft tones with complete confidence in his topic.

"That's enough for today. Don't forget Friday's test. No laptops allowed."

The students groaned as they gathered their notebooks and texts.

Dani watched them file out before standing. She smiled as she approached Reed. "Mr. Donovan?"

"In the flesh."

"Wonderful. You are a hard man to track down."

"Not so. Office, classroom, home. To what do I owe the pleasure?"

She stuck out her hand. "Dani Richards with Channel 17." His face took on a pasty undertone, a challenge considering how pale he seemed at the front of the class. "What can I do for you?"

"I have a couple questions about your relationship with Renee Thomas. Mind if my photographer comes in?" Dani walked to the door and waved Logan in before Reed responded. "I have a meeting in ten minutes." Reed loosened his tie. "No problem. How long did you know Renee?"

"We met shortly after she moved to town. Maybe seven months."

"How did you meet?"

"A friend of a friend's party, I think." His eyes glazed. "She was an amazing person. Larger than life. Above it all. Worked hard, and partied hard."

"Did you date?"

"As soon as she asked, I jumped. But things cooled pretty quickly. Renee was a woman of hot emotions. She'd lurch from extreme to extreme, and I didn't know where we stood from day to day."

"When was the last time you saw her?"

Reed pulled at his tie and unbuttoned the top button. A line of perspiration dotted his brow. "Last week sometime." "Sometime? Tuesday? Thursday?"

"Wait a minute. Are you trying to pin her murder on me?"

"Why? Did you do it?"

"No! Renee invited me to the show."

Dani stared at Reed as he stepped back. "You mean you went to *Cats* with her?"

He shook his head, then nodded.

"Well, which is it?"

"We were supposed to go together, but she changed her mind, practically pushed me out of the theater. The tickets were in someone else's name."

"Whose name?" Did this man really not understand the kind of information he had?

"Blake? Baker? Something like that. She collected the tickets, and I stood off to the side, out of the way. She walked back with the tickets, but something had changed." Reed stopped as he stared at the wall over Dani's head. He pulled his attention back to her. "Renee'd been all fun and flirty. I thought we might have another chance. But as soon as she had the tickets, she shoved me out the door. Next thing I know, I read in the paper that she's dead."

"Why did you break up?"

"She decided I wasn't good enough for her. She'd found someone famous. Someone who could take her places." He shook his head.

"She didn't think I'd do that for her. She couldn't wait to get out of Lincoln."

"Then why did she buy a house?"

Reed scrunched up his face as he looked at Dani. "She didn't own a house. She lived in an apartment a few blocks off campus."

"No, I've been to her house, up off Thirty-third. She moved in two months ago."

"Sorry. The only times I picked her up or took her home, it was to an apartment behind Twenty-seventh and Vine." He looked at his watch, and jerked straight. "I've got to run." He headed back to the podium and grabbed a soft sided briefcase. He started stacking his notes and overheads.

"One last question. Have the police talked to you yet?"

"No. I've been out of town at a conference."

"Have you told them what happened at the theater?"

"And have them think I killed her? I can't do that." He snatched his bag and slunk out the door.

Dani pulled out her phone.

"Who are you calling?" Logan looked up as he looped a cord around his arm.

"Caleb. He needs to know where to find this joker." She reached his voice mail and left a message. "Let's get out of here. I'd like to stop at my house and check on Job on the way back. Then we have to find her other place. Why have two?" she mused aloud.

They soon pulled behind her house. Tension bled from Dani's muscles as she walked through the gate and up the sidewalk and steps to the door. The knob turned easily in her hand, and she stepped back down a couple of steps.

"Logan, did you forget to lock the door this morning?"

21

Dani stared at Logan as he shook his head. She reached for her cell phone tucked in her purse. Her life had become a race to call the police before something else happened. "Time to call Caleb. Again," Dani whispered.

Logan pushed by her, and she teetered on the stair, fighting to keep her balance physically and emotionally. He strode into the kitchen and ducked into the dining room before reappearing in the hallway.

Dani stepped into the kitchen, the loud tick of Aunt Jayne's clock filling the silence. She shuddered. The silence was too complete. "Where's Job? He hasn't even barked a warning."

Logan poked his head around the basement doorway. "I can't find him."

Ice filled her veins as she reached for the phone. Voice mail picked up, and she sank onto a bar stool.

"Caleb, this is Dani. Please come quickly. Someone's broken in." She sucked in a breath of air and tried to steel her voice. "Logan's here with me."

She hung up, and then dialed 911. The dispatcher came on the line, and Dani leaned on the island. "Can you connect me with Investigator Caleb Jamison? Someone's been in my house."

"I'll page him but can send another car while we find him." The woman's placating voice failed to calm Dani. "Please, I need to talk to him."

Logan reentered the room while Dani gave the woman her address. She hung up and looked at him. "The dispatcher says someone will arrive within five minutes. Find anything?" Logan shoved his hands in his pockets.

"What happened to your laptop?"

"What?" She stood and glanced around the room. She'd left the computer on her island, the last place she'd worked. She'd closed it, but now the open laptop lay splintered on the floor. She kneeled in front of it, reached out to touch it and pulled back. Caleb would want the crime scene techs to examine it. With a shudder, she looked around the room. She saw a red smear on the floor, and her heart froze. She inched toward it. "What do you think this is?"

Logan crouched next to her. "Ketchup? We need to get out of here."

Dani shuddered and backed away from the smear. She scanned the floor, looking for more smudges. "Job? Job? Come on, boy. You're scaring me."

Sirens shattered the silence, followed by a pounding on the front door. "Police. Let us in."

Dani unlocked the door and opened it.

An officer pushed her out of the way as another entered the home and began sweeping each room. Caleb entered behind the first two and rushed to Dani's side. "Are you okay?"

She shook her head as tears streamed down her cheeks. Caleb reached for her, and she snuggled into his embrace. She felt sheltered, as if he'd protect her from whatever might

come. His chin settled on top of her head. With everything standing between them, how could she feel so comforted?

He sighed and tipped her chin up. "Dani, I will keep you safe until we catch the man."

She nodded and swallowed hard. "Can you get ahead of him? Now he's been in my house."

Caleb stiffened, then released her and headed for the kitchen. Dani shivered from the sudden absence of his arms. "Tell me what happened."

She filled him in on coming home and finding the door unlocked, no Job and her laptop shattered on the floor. A coldness shrouded Dani. "Have you found Job?" Her voice pitched higher than normal.

"Not yet. He probably got out and will come home. One of your neighbors will see him and put him in the yard." Caleb leaned against the sink.

"I've had him four days. They probably don't realize I have a dog." Bile climbed her throat and threatened to choke Dani. "I have to get out of here before something else happens." Caleb took a step toward her. "We'll find him."

"Who? Job or the person stalking me? Excuse me a minute." She hurried down the back steps and lost what little food she'd grabbed for lunch. She gathered herself on wobbling legs and hobbled back inside. The satchel of clothes she'd left at Tricia's were dirty and wouldn't be enough if she had to hide for any length of time.

In her room, she pulled a pink rolling suitcase out of the closet. She tossed it on the bed and threw clothes into it, hurling shoes on top of suits still encased in dry cleaning bags. Footsteps echoed up the stairs. "Go away, Caleb. I don't know what he's done to my dog. But I'm not waiting for him to come after me. He'll have to find me first."

She swallowed against the tears clogging her throat. She tipped her chin up and turned to get a sweater from her dresser. She swiped the tears away. She pushed past Caleb and headed to the bathroom for toiletries. Once they were in, she zipped the case shut. When she yanked it off the bed, it hit the floor with a thud.

Someone touched her shoulder and she jumped. She turned, hand at her throat, to find Caleb standing in front of her holding her cell phone. He refused to release it until she dragged her gaze to his.

"Where are you running? I can't protect you if I don't know where you are."

"I'll decide once I'm on the road. Lincoln somewhere." She hesitated, then pulled the phone from his grip.

Caleb frowned. "Running isn't going to accomplish anything."

"Other than keeping me safe? I'll call later." She pulled the suitcase toward the hallway.

He grabbed her shoulder, his hand sliding down her arm. Sparks traced his fingers and she quivered. Memories of his touch caused her to tense. He seemed to sense her response and pulled away. "You can't run far enough, Dani. Let me help."

Dani considered his words, but they did nothing to bring her peace. "You don't have any leads." The words were a harsh statement. She pulled the suitcase to the stairs, until Caleb took it from her and carried it downstairs. "I'll call you tonight. Lock up on your way out."

Caleb grabbed her and pulled her to him. Before she could push away, he leaned down and his lips covered hers. Any thought of protest disappeared in the rush of his nearness. He stepped back, and she stared at him as she touched her lips. "You matter to me, Dani. More than you know. Somehow we'll work through everything."

She shook her head and walked to the rental car. Caleb slipped the suitcase into the trunk. "If you don't call, I'll use your phone to find you."

"How?"

"GPS. Call." The one word was a command she couldn't ignore even as her house shrunk in her rearview mirror.

AT WORK DANI pieced together a story she couldn't remember and then left a voice mail for Kate to call her cell. She left the station and headed for Aunt Jayne's. Her eyes flicked to the rearview mirror periodically. No one matched her lane changes or turns.

The minutes ticked by on her dashboard clock with her no closer to a place to hide. She didn't want to return to Tricia's and put her at risk. That left Aunt Jayne.

She drove to the nursing home and parked as close to the front doors as possible. Maybe the stalker didn't know where Aunt Jayne lived. Dani darted through the front doors. Hearing them whoosh shut behind her, she slowed her step and took a deep breath. The frail man sitting behind the information desk made no effort to stop her. She doubted he'd stop anyone else. Once past the desk, she hurried down a hall looking for the lounge, until she heard a telltale cacophony of voices mixed with a blaring TV.

As she peeked into the room, she looked for Aunt Jayne's familiar form huddled over the quilting frame. The frame leaned against the wall, unused.

"Can I help you, young lady?"

Dani jumped and threw her hand over her heart as the voice rumbled next to her ear. She turned to meet the kind eyes of a man who looked to be in his late seventies. "Maybe you can. I'm looking for my aunt. Jayne Richards."

"Be happy to take you to her. She headed to her room an hour or so ago. Guess the quilters got tired of pushing their needles." He offered his arm with a half bow. "Fred Sorenson at your service."

Dani relaxed and placed her arm through his. "Thank you, Mr. Sorenson."

"No bother. I know ole' Tom ain't a lot of help at the front desk."

As they ambled through several hallways, Mr. Sorenson told her all kinds of tall tales.

"Here you go, missy."

"Thank you." As she watched him, Dani realized she'd forgotten everything while laughing. Some of the darkness had receded. She'd find a way to handle this.

A dim light shone from the corner of the room. Dani rapped on the door before she entered. "Aunt Jayne. It's Dani. Are you up for some company?"

As she walked into the small three-room suite, Aunt Jayne looked up from a crossword puzzle book spread across her lap. "Hello?"

Dani glanced at the puzzle and her smile faded. Aunt Jayne had filled the boxes with meaningless combinations of letters and numbers. Sadness gripped Dani at the realization that her disease had robbed Aunt Jayne of another pleasure. "Hi, Aunt Jayne. It's Dani."

"Do I know you? Who are you?" With each word the older woman's voice rose, and she pushed back against the chair.

"I'm sorry. Maybe I have the wrong room." Dani swallowed against the lump in her throat and backed out the door. She leaned against the hallway wall and fought the tears. She hated Alzheimer's. It had taken Dani's best friend, and left Aunt Jayne a frail, confused shadow of herself. There was no way Dani could stay on a night like tonight. Even a short visit would cause alarm. She swiped at the tears trickling down her cheeks and headed back to the entrance.

Once she was back in her car, she pulled out her phone and stared at it. She didn't have anywhere to go. Her house was out, Aunt Jayne couldn't handle her company, and she couldn't ask Tricia. She flipped open the phone and pressed the power button before she changed her mind. This week continued to force her into a closeness with Caleb she wasn't sure she wanted. She didn't have a choice, no matter how she fought that conclusion. She fiddled with her keys as she waited for him to pick up.

"Dani, where are you? You were supposed to call." His voice sounded weighted down.

"I turned the cell off." She bit her lower lip. "Sorry to worry you."

"Are you okay?" His voice calmed, and she heard a creak as he leaned back in his chair.

"No. I came to Aunt Jayne's, but she's not having a good night. I'm out of ideas and options." Dani wiped a tear from her lashes. "I'm ready to head back downtown, probably to the Cornhusker Hotel."

Caleb was silent a moment. "Sure you don't want reinforcements?"

"You need your sleep. I'll be fine."

Dani heard a clink, like he'd sat up. "You are stubborn. And I'm not sure the Cornhusker's a good idea."

"Why not?"

"He always seems a step ahead of you. He's probably guessed you won't stay at your house tonight and may check hotels, looking for you." He cleared his throat, then paused. "I've got an idea. Come meet me at the station on Twenty-seventh." "Why? What's your idea?" A bad feeling snaked through Dani. She didn't know what he was going to say, but feared she wouldn't like it.

22

The hum of a scanner filtered behind him as Caleb considered how to frame his solution. She needed sleep and he needed to know she was safe. A hotel wasn't the answer—this stalker had proved he would find her anywhere. The only way to protect her was to have her with him. He could imagine her reaction, and hoped she'd listen long enough to hear that Tricia would join them.

"We'll go to my cabin."

She sputtered, and he could imagine the mask of anger that would be on her face. Could she find a way to trust him? That question roiled through him, even as he knew this was the best solution.

"Dani, Tricia will meet us there. It's the only place the stalker wouldn't think to look for you. I haven't been there much for the last week, and it's secluded."

"I could leave town." Her tone was so cold he almost looked for his jacket.

"If you were going to run, you would have already done that. You won't. It's not how you approach life."

"No, that's all you."

Caleb grimaced at the accusation that hit too close to home. If she only knew how much he regretted that—even more now that he knew he had a little girl running around calling someone else Daddy. A little girl who probably looked a lot like Dani, with pretty blond hair twisted in braids and blue eyes sparkling with life. Maybe he should let her go to the Cornhusker. Let her handle this on her own like she'd handled the pregnancy. No, as long as this case remained active, he was responsible for her. Regardless of whether either of them liked it.

"Dani, this isn't about us or the past. It's about keeping you safe until we catch the stalker."

"Yeah, you've always been the safe choice." Caleb waited— she had to come around. There were no options. "Fine. I'll be there in ten minutes."

She hung up before he could respond, and Caleb tipped his chair back. He ran his hands through his hair. Dani would be spitting mad, and he would be the sole target. Maybe Tricia would temper her. If not, he'd put up with the attitude to protect her.

"Good news, boss?" Westmont sat and stared at Caleb.

"No. But I've got guard duty on Miss Richards tonight."

Westmont rolled his eyes. "Sounds like a rough job. Want me to do it?"

"Sorry, but I can't." Trust her to anyone else, that is. Much as he liked Westmont, this was something he had to do. "I'll be at the cabin if you need me. Otherwise, let's collect Baker first thing in the morning and have another chat. I'll wait for her out front."

"See you in the morning."

Caleb grabbed his keys and sports jacket and headed out the front. He only had to wait a minute before Dani pulled into the lot. She threw the car in Park.

"I don't even want to know how many laws you broke getting here."

The car shook as she slammed the door. "You listen to me, Caleb Jamison. I am only going with you because I am desperate. Don't even think this is some kind of rendezvous. So help me, if you try anything.

"My, we become violent under stress, don't we?" He nodded at a passing officer who'd paused out of Dani's line of sight with his hand on his gun. "Don't worry, this has nothing to do with us. And everything to do with keeping you safe."

She stared at him angrily. "You expect me to believe you offer every stalking victim a free night at your cabin?"

"I've never made this offer before. Don't forget, Tricia will be there to protect you from me."

She bit her lower lip and looked away. Her shoulders slumped, and he couldn't decide whether to pull her toward him or throttle her. Dani seemed to reach a decision and opened her eyes. "Okay, I'll come. But the moment you try anything, I'm out of there and you will never see me again."

"If you're done yelling, I'm going to get in my car and you can follow me." She stared at him as if he'd gone crazy, so he spun and hustled to his car. He hopped in and pulled his next to hers. "Ready?"

Dani threw her arms in the air and stormed to her car. They just needed to get through the night without killing each other.

THE HEADLIGHTS MADE it easy to follow Caleb, even as she questioned her sanity with each mile. It had been years since she'd visited Branched Oak—long enough to forget how remote the area was.

Dani pushed back memories of that night ten years earlier.

She'd been a kid overly impressed with the idea a star football player wanted to spend time with her, told her she was special. She was older now and knew what she wanted from life. Caleb had also grown up with the years. One minute she wanted to push the new Caleb into the past next to the old one. The next she wasn't sure. Even as she'd argued with him in the parking lot, a large part of her had craved the shelter of his arms.

The road twisted to the right again, and she followed Caleb into a driveway. A small log cabin stood at the end of the driveway. Tricia's cream Mercedes was pulled to one side of the driveway.

Caleb climbed out of his car. "Here we are. Home sweet home."

Dani grabbed her bag and stared at the door. Caleb slipped the bag from her hand.

"Come in. I have a feeling Tricia has something waiting for us."

She wanted to follow, but her muscles refused to cooperate. She stood locked in place, staring at a red door.

"Dani? You can relax now. You're safe. The stalker has no idea where you are unless he happens to be driving out here right now and sees you standing here."

Caleb opened the door and switched on a lamp. Soft light glowed in the living room. She was surprised to see a leather recliner and a big screen TV along with an Oriental rug and striped couch. Tricia glanced up from her spot on the couch, pushing a file out of her lap.

"Hey, guys. Would you like something to eat, Dani? I brought some ice cream. You never know what Caleb will have on hand."

"One scoop sounds good."

Caleb headed down the hallway. "The bedroom and guest bedroom are down here. The first door is my room." He opened the door. Two twin beds flanked built-in bookcases. A duffel bag sat on top of one, and Caleb put her suitcase on the other. "This will work fine. Thanks, Caleb. Let's get that ice cream." Three bowls waited on the table, one overflowing with four heaping scoops. Dani picked at her bowl while Tricia and Caleb bantered. She pushed her bowl away and stifled a yawn. "I'm heading to bed. Good night."

Caleb nodded, but focused on the table, continuing to ignore Dani. What was he thinking?

CALEB LISTENED to Dani slip down the hallway, but couldn't shake the darkness he felt to say good night. After the door closed, Tricia reached for his hand.

"How are you doing?"

"This is the first time in days I've had time to think about what

Dani did. She decided I shouldn't get to be a father." Her grasp tightened on his. "I'm sorry."

"I didn't deserve that. I don't know anything about the family she chose. Did she do any kind of investigation into them? Are they good people?"

"There had to be a home study. You know it wasn't an easy decision for her either."

"Maybe. But she's had ten years to deal with it. I've only had a couple days. I'm so angry. And then the next minute I want to see if we can start all over again." He pulled his hand free and ran it over his face.

"I don't know, Caleb. Dani did what she thought she had to do. Can you see her parents letting her raise a baby or raising it for her?"

No, they'd never seemed overly supportive to him. That was the problem. When he could approach the situation rationally, he knew she'd had no other choice. But it had been his daughter.

"You've got to turn this over to God. Don't let this make you bitter, Caleb. Grieve, deal with it, but do all that with Him." He nodded and swallowed around the boulder in his throat. "Thanks, Tricia."

"That's what baby sisters are for. Good night."

Once he was alone, Caleb buried his head in his hands. He had to push through this. Whatever it took.

23

Thursday morning, the sizzle of bacon and scent of brewing coffee pulled Caleb from his sleep. Where was he? He opened his eyes and saw his living room. He must have fallen asleep on the couch. He startled to his feet. He was supposed to guard Dani and Tricia last night.

"Morning." Tricia flipped something on the stove. Dani stood next to her, nursing a cup of what smelled like coffee. She looked so natural and relaxed standing there, he smiled.

"Good morning."

She turned toward him. A shy smile tipped her lips. "Hey. Tricia thought you might want some breakfast before we headed to work."

"Smells good, though I'm surprised you gals found anything. I haven't been home much."

"Sit down. The coffee's hot."

"And don't forget the pancakes on the table." Tricia wiped her forehead. "I slaved over those beauties."

Breakfast passed in a quick blur. It felt like some switch had flipped in his attitude toward Dani. It could only be the fruit of hours wrestling with God. An hour later they left, headed back to the unknown. Now Caleb's thoughts raced as he strode into the conference room.

Last night he'd stayed awake too long as he'd argued with God about why he couldn't release his anger. Yet the more he argued, the more he knew he had to forgive. Just like she'd have to forgive him at some point if they were to move ahead. He'd ended the night praying for wisdom to guide her safely through whatever was still coming.

Westmont had secured her phone records from the telephone company. Caleb settled at the conference table and reviewed the list of calls while he waited for the others to take a seat. Based on the list, Dani couldn't have slept in almost a week. The calls had been that constant.

She'd hidden the magnitude of the problem. Now all calls to her number automatically forwarded to the station.

"Earth to grand Pumba." Westmont threw a paper clip from across the table. Caleb looked up from the file and frowned. "What do you have?"

Denimore reported on forwarded calls. "A couple look promising. I'll track down the callers this morning."

Westmont flipped through the phone records. "She didn't get many calls at all until the night of the murder. The stalker is connected. My guess? The stalker and murderer are the same."

"Agreed. Westmont, we'll interview Baker. Denimore, grab someone and track your leads. If the culprit's not Baker, I want to know why and who it might be as soon as possible. If Baker's our man, I want enough evidence to get him on this murder before something else happens." Caleb downed a Coke and aspirin. He grabbed his sports coat and stood.

He heard Todd's lumbering steps behind him. Caleb planned the interview while he prayed Dani was okay.

A short while later an officer settled Baker in a chair next to his attorney behind the battered metal table of the interrogation room. Caleb wondered if Baker understood his situation. Last time they talked, Baker had treated the interview like a game.

Showtime.

He pushed the door open, throwing his file on the table as he entered. Baker jumped. Caleb settled down in his chair and pulled a mini tape recorder from his pocket and pushed the record button.

"Mr. Baker. Nice to see you again."

"Can we get to the point? I have a boss expecting me." The words bordered on open hostility.

"I have some follow up questions. We'll let you call Channel 17 later. Your attorney is here, correct ?"

"Yes."

"And you've had an opportunity to consult with your attorney?"

"Yes." Baker looked at his lawyer, an uninspiring middle- aged man who pushed a comb over across his forehead.

Caleb read Baker his Miranda rights. "Let's start with your relationship with Renee Thomas."

"We didn't have a relationship." Baker's voice boomed in the small room.

'That's not what you told me last week."

"Don't distort my words. We were at the same football game, and she had her photo taken with me. That's it." Baker rubbed his nose as he talked.

Caleb settled back and stared. If he waited long enough, the stare wore down most people who lied.

Baker looked from his attorney to Caleb. Disgust clouded across his face as his lawyer doodled on a legal pad. "What am I paying you for? Remind me to fire you."

The attorney rolled his eyes and kept sketching.

Caleb made a note to get the guy's name. With his kind of help, they'd crack cases faster. Of course, if convictions got thrown out for ineffective assistance of counsel, it wouldn't make his job easier.

Baker pinched his nose as he looked at the table. "Don't you understand?"

"It's simple. All I want is the truth. I won't quit asking until that's what you tell me."

"She was a kid. She acted like I was a celebrity. Called all the time until I agreed to meet her for lunch."

Caleb studied his face. His pinching the bridge of his nose, the way he refused to look at Caleb, all indicated Baker lied. "What happened after lunch?" Silence. "If you won't tell me about you and Renee, then I'll hold you awhile."

"You can't do that." Baker looked at his attorney.

"If he can prove you're material to the case, he can."

"I can do that and will hold you until I can prove you're lying. While you decide what the truth is, let me tell you what I know. One, you had a relationship with Miss Thomas. Two, you sold her a house below market value. Three, you purchased her theater ticket. Oh, and I shouldn't forget your wife knew nothing about any of this until we talked to her earlier this morning."

"I didn't kill her."

"So you admit you had a relationship." Baker shrugged. "Give me something to believe. Right now everything is stacked against you."

"You heard the man." Mr. Attorney looked up from the page that now contained an elaborate depiction of Lady Justice. "Tell him the truth, and we'll get you out of here."

"But my wife will leave me." Baker stiffened. "I can't let that happen. Do you know what an anchor makes in a town this size? Not enough. Her inheritance is our retirement. It'll put our kids through college."

"You should have thought of that before the affair. And why come to Lincoln if the pay's so bad?"

"Things got out of hand in Denver. I acquired a couple of fans who deluded themselves into believing they loved me. And that I loved them. One threatened my family, so we left." "Stalking. Did you do anything about it?"

"Other than useless protective orders and getting a gun? No. How do you fight a threat like that?"

"I'll check that. Back to Renee." Caleb pulled a pad of paper from his folder. He itched to write something that resembled truth. "*Did* you have a relationship with her?" Baker examined his well-manicured fingers where they twitched on the table. "Yes. Renee and I were involved." Caleb picked up his pen. A few more honest answers and he'd have a better feel for whether Baker was involved in her murder beyond just looking guilty. "How long did you know her?" "We met at a football game. She knew the man who hosted the tailgate I attended, and we crossed paths."

"Why did you sell her the house?"

"We needed a place to meet, and she hated apartment life. Somehow she knew about the house and nagged until I gave in. It didn't hurt I wanted to keep her in Lincoln."

"What did your wife think?"

"All I told her was I'd found a buyer. She trusted me. And I blamed the rest on a journalist's schedule."

Caleb sat back and listened as Baker talked. The relationship had the on-again, off-again characteristic of convenience. They could go a week or two without seeing each other, and then she'd call and it'd flame again.

"Did you ever think about your wife and children?" "Why else do you think we stopped for a week or two?" Caleb fought his disgust at Baker's attitude that his attempts to end it somehow made him noble. "So you killed her to end the relationship?"

"No."

Baker's attorney eyed Caleb. "Careful, Officer. You're approaching the line where I will advise my client to stop talking."

"Then I'll walk him to a cell."

"Not without an arrest warrant. Even so, I'd advise you to focus on the relevant and not hurl accusations."

The attorney had some backbone after all. "If you didn't kill her, who did? You're a smart man. Surely you have some theories."

Baker nodded. "It wasn't me. And I wasn't there."

"Stop right there. A witness places you at the theater during Act I. One problem with your job, Mr. Baker, people notice you." Baker leaned forward, his back ramrod straight as he did. "Then you should understand this. When I was with Renee, *she* was who people saw. She had a magnetic personality and amazing beauty. I disappeared when I was with her. She loved that fact."

"If that's the way you felt, why stay? Come on, you have a beautiful wife at home."

"Who's told me she'd leave if I ever got involved and it became public knowledge."

"I guess that's happened." The realization you'll always be caught in your sin seared Caleb's mind. Baker was a walking example.

"Yes."

"The only way to help yourself out of jail is to tell me who killed Renee."

"She didn't talk about herself. And when she did I didn't understand. It was all chemistry and research." Baker spread his palms in front of him. "She mentioned a guy who gave her trouble at school."

"Can you be any more specific about him?"

"No. I tuned her out when she whined about him."

Caleb shook his head. Listening might have saved her life.

24

Vinnie Carloni? Dani stared at the assignment board, waiting for the name to morph into Logan Collins. She and the kid videographer would spend the morning and early afternoon in the Haymarket. Nothing like covering a grade school anti-drug rally to make her question her sanity and wish she was back at Caleb's cabin. Between Tricia and Caleb, she'd been safe from all but her thoughts. She imagined their daughter joining him at the breakfast table. Dani shook her head to clear the vision. It was too late for what might have been.

Tori walked by. "Snap out of it, Dani. You've beat that murder into the ground."

"The police are questioning Phil."

"But they haven't arrested him. Time to do some real reporting." She flounced toward her desk.

Dani made a face at Tori's back, and then grabbed the press release and schedule from LeAnn at the assignment desk. With Vinnie, it was good the story was small. Maybe this time he'd frame the shots properly. She walked to her desk. Time to get her head back in the game.

Maybe Tori was right. Maybe she'd become so focused on the

murder, she couldn't see what was in front of her anymore. Dani couldn't shake an unsettling feeling. She'd promised she'd find Renee's murderer. And she meant it, even if she did it on her time. And as long as someone stalked her because of the murder, she wouldn't quit.

Vinnie, a skinny kid right out of college, hovered outside her cube. "Ready, Miss Richards?"

Rolling her eyes, Dani stood. "Let's get this over with."

"Yes, ma'am."

"Make sure you get plenty of b-roll. We've got four newscasts to cover. Lots of school groups will be there, and you know how Kate likes kids."

"Yeah, parents guaranteed to watch the news."

"You've got it."

Dani followed Vinnie to a car. The Haymarket was tucked between Ninth Street and the train tracks. The area had been revitalized in the last twenty years, evolving into a quaint area filled with cute shops and great restaurants. They'd follow kids from the Haymarket to the football stadium. That is if Vinnie could find a parking spot. They found the neighborhood overrun with school buses and groups of kids and chaperones.

"Why don't you park behind the ice cream shop. We can walk from there."

Each spring the university football coach held an anti-drug rally associated with the spring football game. Many of the players participated, and the kids loved the chance to be on the revered football field. The kids formed a sea of red and white shirts, reflecting the university's colors.

"Come on, Vinnie." Dani emerged from the car and joined the flow of groups hiking up the hill toward the stadium. Her first foray into the hallowed halls of Memorial Stadium would be with a crowd of kids. If only she understood the fervor that surrounded football.

Up ahead, a dark head bobbed above the sea, a Channel 17 baseball cap shoved on his head. He turned and Dani stopped. The man looked a lot like Phil Baker. What was he doing here? He should be at the station, prepping for the evening shows. The man ambled along with a group, and Dani rushed to catch up. She tried to remember if Phil had any assignments, but drew a blank. She certainly couldn't see him enjoying kiddie time. He favored high society and political events, and would find children's features beneath his status as head anchor.

A little boy jostled against her and then stumbled. His knees and hands collided with the sidewalk, and he started to cry.

"Here. Let me help you up."

He worried his lower Up as tears trailed down his cheeks. Dani pulled him to his feet, and the boy rushed ahead to catch up with his group. Vinnie was far behind her, and Phil had now slipped to the side. Her glance collided with his, and she felt ice form in her stomach. He'd pulled the cap low over his forehead and his eyes were hooded. He ducked up the stairs and into a shop.

Dani stared after him. No question he'd dared her to follow him. She glanced over her shoulder at Vinnie and waved. He nodded at her and shrugged. Guess he'd catch up eventually. *Don't go anywhere alone, Dani.* Caleb's words filled her mind, but Caleb wasn't here.

Taking a deep breath, Dani hurried up the stairs and stepped into the building. Row after row of antiques filled the cavernous structure that looked as though it had once been a warehouse. The old wooden floors squeaked with each step she took. Dust hung in the air. She pulled her sunglasses to the top of her head and waited for her eyes to adjust to the dim light.

Movement caught her eye, and she watched Phil slip toward the back.

"Can I help you?" A matronly woman with round glasses smiled at her from behind a large wooden counter.

"I'm just looking."

The woman frowned. "The last group broke a set of dishes. Break it and you pay for it."

Dani nodded and went down the aisle. What a ray of sunshine. Now, where had Baker gone?

❧

WESTMONT STARED AT THE WHITEBOARD, while Caleb didn't need the whiteboard to tell him what his gut knew. Phil Baker was his only suspect, and a slippery one. That interview hadn't helped. Any.

"Baker bought the tickets, but paid cash."

Todd nodded. "No one will confirm he was at the theater."

"We've got the usher."

"Who won't stand up under intense questioning by a good defense attorney and is in the hospital. Baker had a relationship with Renee."

"That we can only surmise because of a photo and the fact he sold her the house. He admits they had an affair, but not that they were together at the time of the murder." Caleb rubbed the back of his neck. "The guy knows how to dance."

"A regular Arthur Murray graduate. Why kill her? And why Thursday night?"

Caleb shook his head. "I don't know. Her boyfriend cooperate yet?"

"He's dodging us. Doesn't he get that it makes him look guilty? Whatever happened to helping the police?"

"Too many crime shows." Everybody assumed they needed an attorney. And all he wanted was a few facts. The kind that stood up in court.

Westmont headed toward the door. "Donovan's got a class until eleven forty-five. I'll be waiting."

Caleb nodded, something niggling at the edges of his mind. He turned to the box of files he'd brought back from Renee's house. His finger ran across the tabs. He'd been through them. Westmont and Denimore had searched them, too. He didn't know what he expected to find, just that he had to do something.

Satellite. Credit Card. House. He pulled each out. File after file, nothing new jumped out at him. He shoved the last file in the box and walked to the break room. He was missing something.

If he didn't piece it together, something would happen to Dani.

His gut twisted. He'd lost a daughter. He would not lose Dani. Not again.

"You okay, Caleb?" Rikki walked past him to the refrigerator.

"Sure." He tried to grin.

"Looks like you could use some prayer. You'll figure it out."

The captain walked in.

"Figure what out?"

"How to protect a certain young lady and solve a murder." Rikki winked at him and walked out.

The captain's deep voice carried as if he addressed a crowd. "Need any help, Jamison?"

"No. I'm on it." Caleb hurried back to the conference room before the captain could probe too deeply. He didn't have time to answer questions.

A rap sounded on the open door.

Caleb looked up to see Nate Winslow, a crime scene tech from the murder. The kid was a science whiz but always looked as if he'd sucked a lemon. "What have you got for me?" "Preliminary results. Too many people in and out of that box the night of the incident to get clean fibers. Frankly, it would be hard to nail down what was from that night and prior nights. However, we've classified most of them, and we'll be able to match anything you get for us."

Great. Now all he needed was a warrant to search Baker's closet. "Anything stand out?"

"Not from the fibers collected from the carpet and seats. However, from Miss Thomas herself, we found a couple of interesting things. First, we have a silk fiber that is likely from a red tie. That fiber was attached to the back of her dress, about shoulder height."

"Can you narrow it down?"

"Not really, but we'll match it."

"The good news."

Nate blew a breath through his teeth in a huff. "Patience is a virtue."

"Not in a murder investigation."

"Fine. There were also two black hairs, human and fresh, near her. Good news is there was enough root to run a DNA test. Bad news, it'll take weeks to get the results back. Once we do, you might get a hit."

Make that highly unlikely unless the sample belonged to a convicted felon already in the system.

"I thought you might like this, too." Nate pulled out a pocket-size calendar tucked inside a Ziploc bag.

Caleb reached for it and turned it over. Small enough to fit in a jacket pocket, there was nothing remarkable about it. He cocked an eyebrow and motioned Nate to continue.

"It was in one of the boxes we collected from the victim's home. It's taken us a few days to process everything we collected, but this looks like her calendar." Nate shrugged.

Leave it to Nate to leave the most important thing for last. "Prints run on it?"

"Yep. Looks like all of them are the victim's. It's this year's, but maybe it'll help."

Caleb set the bag down and pulled on a pair of gloves. Carefully, he opened the bag and tugged out the small book. He flipped through the weeks, scanning carefully. "Bingo."

25

A floorboard creaked down the hall. A flash of indecision stopped Dani in her tracks. Vinnie still hadn't caught up with her, and Phil had disappeared. Maybe she should follow Caleb's advice and stick close to others for a while. How many nights did she really want to spend at other people's houses? Not many. She pulled out her cell phone and dialed the station. The receptionist patched her through to the assignment desk. Dani tapped her toe as she waited for LeAnn to answer.

"Hey, LeAnn. Quick question. Is Phil in? I have a question about this story." She pressed the phone closer to her ear, trying to hear LeAnn's words through the static. "Wait, let me step outside." She rushed from the building and waved at Vinnie as he huffed to the stairs. "Can you say that again? Phil's been released by the police? He's headed back to the station?"

The door behind her opened, and Dani stumbled forward as someone bumped into her. Vinnie steadied her, and she turned. An elderly woman teetered toward the stairs.

"So sorry."

"No problem," Dani mumbled. She beckoned Vinnie to follow

her. "I need to check something inside." She hurried back inside and down the aisle toward the rear. As she walked, she watched for Phil.

A muffled whistle carried from the back, and she hurried toward the sound. The off-key tune got louder. She turned in to a booth, and bounced into an antique desk. Her side smarted from the imprint of a drawer knob.

"Are you okay?" The man with the Channel 17 hat secured her with a sure grip. His eyes filled with concern.

"I'm fine. Sorry." She backed away from him. How had she ever thought he looked like Phil? Except for the dark hair and Channel 17 hat, he looked nothing like Phil. Phil stood taller and carried more muscle than this guy. And she'd never seen Phil in a baseball cap. Tori was right. It was time to get her head back in her job before she did something stupid.

"Vinnie?" She scurried out of the booth and found Vinnie at the front of the store. She pushed him toward the door. "Let's rush and catch up with those kids." Maybe she could salvage the assignment.

An hour later, Vinnie packed up his equipment. The rally had passed swiftly as the children repeated the pledge the starting quarterback read. She'd interviewed a dozen excited kids and coaxed answers out of them. The stories would work, though not her usual hard-edged reporting. Her eyes had filled each time she'd seen a young girl with blond hair and green eyes. Life was supremely unfair. She'd lived for years with the memory of her daughter pushed far to the side. Now one week with Caleb, and every thought seemed to include her and other what-ifs from her life.

"Ready, Miss Richards?"

"Let's get back." As if she'd ever be ready for stories like this. She climbed in the car while Vinnie stowed the gear. By the time they reached the station, she had the packages drafted and ready to read. "Set me up in an audio booth, please." She walked back to her cube, scanning the newsroom for Phil. His office was dark, and she couldn't see him anywhere. "LeAnn, has Phil shown up?"

"Nope. He'll waltz in at the last minute."

"And pull off the newscast."

"He always does." The scanners blared to life, and LeAnn turned back to them.

Vinnie waved at Dani and motioned toward the audio booth. A pounding in her head made her want to curl up under her desk and hide. Instead, she cut the audio and tossed the tape to Vinnie with instructions on what video and sound bites to use. She headed back to her computer.

Her pocket vibrated, and Dani jumped. She tugged her phone from her jacket pocket. The number on the display was unfamiliar, but an envelope icon flashed in the corner. Dread coiled around her middle.

Her fingers shook as she opened the phone and pulled up the message. A grainy picture of Aunt Jayne filled the tiny screen. Her grip tightened on the phone as a strange stillness settled over her. She tried to take a breath, but her body ignored her mind's instructions. All she could do was stare at the picture. What had she done?

Dani dashed to the bathroom and locked the door. A moan echoed against the tiled walls.

She studied the picture again. Nothing looked familiar in the dark shadows behind Aunt Jayne's huddled form. The phone fell from Dani's grip and bounced on the floor. Her pale reflection in the mirror mimicked her motions as Dani splashed cold water on her face. *Steady, girl. Don't lose control now.* Her knees ignored her instructions and buckled.

She had to call Caleb and go find Aunt Jayne before something happened.

Dani pulled herself up and grabbed a paper towel from the dispenser. Dread coiled in her stomach. He had Aunt Jayne, the only person she would willingly trade her life for.

Stooping, Dani grabbed the phone and slipped from the restroom. She needed help, since she couldn't identify where her aunt was. Before she could place a call, her phone shimmied again, and she hit the green button. "Hello."

Heavy breathing filled her ear.

"I know you're there. Say something or leave me alone." Heads popped up from around the newsroom, watching with blatant curiosity. Dani frowned. This wasn't a conversation for them to overhear. She pushed through the outside door, and a blast of cold air hit her in the face. "Well? I'll hang up then." "Those are brave words, little girl." A trickle of fear crept down her spine.

"You have twenty minutes to meet me, or your dear auntie..." "How do I know you haven't already killed her?" A tremor filled her voice at the thought.

"You don't. But you can't afford to be wrong."

Her fingers trembled, and she clutched the phone tighter. "Where should I meet you?"

"Look at the photo."

"I don't know where you took it." A death grip squeezed her. "Where's camera boy? How about lover boy? Can't they protect you?"

"Caleb will find you."

"No, he's incapable. Even when I'm in plain sight." He inhaled, and it felt as if he sucked the air out of her lungs into his. "You have your clue. Fifteen minutes."

"Wait." All she heard was a click. "No. I don't understand." Tears slid unchecked down her cheeks.

Look at the picture. She fumbled with her phone until she pulled up the grainy image of Aunt Jayne. "There has to be something here," she groaned. Her eyes teared as she strained to see every detail. Then she noticed the frame hanging on the wall behind her aunt. She swiped her eyes with the back of her hand and squinted. She'd seen it somewhere before.

Dani struggled to her feet as it hit her. The framed cross stitch had hung in Aunt Jayne's living room for years.

She ran to the Neon. Only twelve minutes. It was a long shot. Could it be that simple? If he waited in her house, she might make it in time.

Caleb. She had to reach him. Let him know what was happening. She frantically dialed his number, once, twice, but her fingers didn't cooperate. Finally, she pulled up the right number, but the call went straight to voice mail. Next she called 911. The dispatcher told her to wait for officers. An impossible request if Aunt Jayne was in there and in danger.

Dani steeled herself. She could see her house up a block and felt exposed. Could he see her already? Dani pulled to the side of the road before entering the alley. If she parked on the street, somebody might notice the car.

She picked up her phone. She had less than a minute to try Caleb again. She dialed quickly and froze when voice mail picked up again. Where was he?

"Caleb, the stalker has Aunt Jayne at my house. Please hurry."

Next, she dialed Tricia's house and left another message. Still no officer at the house. She'd have to go in alone.

She called dispatch and asked for Caleb. She waited on hold as minutes ticked away. The dispatcher patched her through to Westmont.

"What's up, Dani?"

"I need Caleb."

"He stepped out but should be back soon."

"Tell him I'm at my house. The stalker has Aunt Jayne, and if I don't get in there now, he'll kill her."

A muted roar filled the car. "Don't do it, Dani. Wait for us to get there."

"It's too late." She closed the phone and glanced in the rearview mirror. She closed her eyes and tried to wipe the fear from her face.

Time was up.

She tucked the cell phone in her pocket. The stalker had won. Maybe the cavalry would arrive in time. But if he did something to Aunt Jayne, it wouldn't matter. Dani had to try to save her.

After she climbed out of the car, Dani tucked the keys under the driver's side mat and left it unlocked.

Rather than enter the house from the back, Dani walked to the front door. She took a deep breath. Ordered her stomach to stop roiling. She stepped to the side, gagged, but nothing came. She forced herself upright and climbed the stairs. Lifting her hand, she hesitated before twisting the knob.

Heavy footsteps echoed down the hallway and through the wood.

She braced herself as she opened the door. The blood drained from her face. He caught her roughly under the arms.

"Glad you could join us."

26

S teering his unmarked police car through traffic on Sixteenth Street, an unsettled feeling churned through Caleb. He prayed for wisdom as his head pounded.

His phone had been awfully quiet. He grabbed it and groaned. Battery dead. Again. He pulled the cord out and plugged it in. It blipped to life and dinged to indicate a message.

His cell phone rang. Flipping it open, he pulled it to his ear. "Jamison."

"Hey, boss," Westmont said. "Get to Dani's house now."

"Why?"

"She's headed there to meet her stalker. He claims to have her aunt."

Caleb rubbed his temple. If it was true, the stalker had nailed Dani. He doubted she could live with herself if something happened to her aunt. Acid burned in his stomach. "When did she call?"

"Fifteen minutes ago."

"Why didn't you call me?" The words exploded from Caleb.

"Have been. Phone run out of juice again?"

"She was headed home?"

"That's what she said." Westmont sighed. "She didn't give me a chance to talk her out of it. I tried. I sent a car that way. Denimore and I are heading out, too."

Caleb shook his head. "Find her. Now." Caleb threw his phone back on the passenger seat. At the next intersection he flipped on his emergency lights and made a U-turn.

If he closed his eyes, he saw fingers tighten around Dani's slender neck. She could be in Baker's hands already. It had to be Baker, yet it felt like a faceless phantom played with her, controlled her with his messages. Caleb's inability to protect her paralyzed him.

He reached for the phone and tried Dani's number. It rang and rang, but she didn't answer. He called dispatch next. Caleb's jaw clenched so tightly his teeth grated. Where was she? Did Baker already have her?

As the car flew down the road, he prayed with all his might that God would protect Dani. And that he wouldn't be too late.

～

DANI WINCED when Phil grabbed her arm and pulled her through the doorway. As he tugged her down the hall, she stumbled. Knowledge of his plans seeped into her. She looked around, desperate for a weapon and a glimpse of Aunt Jayne. "Where is she, you monster? Where are you hiding her?" "Who? Your precious auntie? Brilliant stroke, wasn't it? You would have put me off if I threatened anyone else, but not if it was poor demented Jayne."

Heat exploded through her. She flailed at him, trying to twist from his death grip. She grabbed for something, anything she could use as a weapon.

He threw her in a chair at the dining room table. Phil pulled a gun from his pocket and took a seat across the table. "Don't even think of moving."

"Where is she?" She lurched out of the chair.

He pointed the gun at her. "I will use this if you insist." Dani sank onto the unforgiving wood chair. Her gaze darted around the room and into the kitchen, searching for Aunt Jayne.

"Time for us to get better acquainted." His words stretched into silence.

What did he want? Dani froze in place until the image of Aunt Jayne flung against the couch pushed her past her fear. She had to find Aunt Jayne. She could almost feel the evil in the room as a breath tickled her ear.

He stared at Dani's cell phone as it rang on the table. While he waited, he settled back in the dining room chair. The last ring echoed off the walls. "May I?"

Dani nodded mutely and watched as he picked it up. Her gaze landed on a thin rope next to his gun on the tabletop. She choked as fear coiled around her. Once she saw it, she couldn't look anywhere else.

He looked up and caught her staring at the rope. "Wonder why you're here? It's really simple. I couldn't share Renee with anyone. She was the most luminous person I've ever known. The love we shared was passionate and deep."

"And you killed her." Dani shook her head. "Do you have any idea how crazy that sounds? Renee had several boyfriends. That doesn't sound like love."

Phil stiffened at her words. "Ours was a special love." He waved the gun. "I have all the power. Just like with Renee. She flaunted her new boyfriend in my face." He snorted. "Look where that got her."

"You don't have to do this." The words sounded as if they came from a scared little girl rather than a professional who made a living from her well-modulated voice.

He snorted and opened the phone.

"Looks like lover boy called. You don't think he's concerned, do you?" He slipped the phone in his pocket, and then leaned on the table. "It's too little, too late. Time to leave."

27

Caleb tuned out the siren as its wail parted cars. He tightened his hold on the steering wheel. Twenty-four hours. That's all that mattered. That's all he could focus on right now. He had to treat this like any kidnapping with the twenty four hour deadline.

Start at her house. Confirm she wasn't there. Baker wouldn't stay in such an obvious place. So where would he go?

He punched Logan's number into his phone. "Meet me outside the station in two minutes. I need your expertise."

Caleb swung into the Channel 17 parking lot and pulled to a quick stop. Logan hustled out and slid into the passenger seat. "Where's Baker?"

"Called in sick. He won't be back until tomorrow or the next day."

"Does he have a second home or retreat?"

"Why?"

Caleb whipped the car back on Vine, headed west toward Dani's house. If the lights cooperated he'd be there in minutes. "Phil's my best guess for who has her. Patrol cars are headed to his house. I don't expect him to be there."

"I can't think with that siren roaring." Caleb flipped the switch. Silence filled the car.

"There's his grandfather's cabin at the lake."

"Where?"

Logan screwed up his face and strummed his fingers against the door. "Near Branched Oak." He grabbed a scrap of paper and began writing. He finished and shoved the paper at Caleb. "This should get you close if you need it."

"Thanks. We'll check Dani's house first, then head to the cabin." Caleb reached across Logan and pulled two power bars out of his glove box. "Eat this—it'll keep you alert through stress." He tore open his bar and forced himself to eat even as it fell like lead in his stomach.

As he reached for a second bar, Logan started laughing.

"What?"

"You still eat like crazy when you're under stress."

"At least it's energy bars rather than onion rings." His stomach rebelled. The last time he'd had those was with Dani. Another minute rolled by on the dashboard clock. Caleb rubbed his temples with one hand while passing a semi. The light changed to red, and Caleb raced through it. A blue SUV barreled into view, the driver yakking on his phone.

Metal ground against metal. Logan grunted. The SUV pushed the car into another vehicle. Caleb jerked forward a split second until his seat belt locked. Logan grabbed his shoulder and groaned.

Caleb shook his head to clear the edges of confusion. He flipped on his lights and watched the driver's eyes widen. "Yeah. Picked the wrong car to hit." He reached for the radio and called in the accident. "Rikki, get someone here quickly. Logan needs an ambulance, and I need another car. Now."

The dashboard clock blazed the time. Caleb edged out of the car and paced. The other driver glanced at him, then slid down in his seat. Caleb looked everywhere for the squad car. It pulled in next to his smashed vehicle, sirens blaring and lights flashing. A portly uniformed officer hopped out. "She's all yours."

"Thanks." Caleb collapsed into the passenger seat. "Thirty- fourth and Vine. Now!"

"Officer John Osborne, sir."

"Great. Drive."

DANI SHIVERED as he stood and walked around the table. Emptiness replaced the life that usually flashed in Phil's eyes. It was as if he looked through her to someone else. As another tremor shook her frame, she tore her gaze from his and looked at the walls. *Find rest, O my soul, in God alone; my hope comes from Him. He alone is my rock and my salvation.* The words scripted along the wall drew her with hope.

I need some hope, God. Hope that Aunt Jayne is alive. Hope I won't die today.

As he approached, Dani scooted her chair back. Heard the harsh scrape of wood on wood. His manicured hands pulled her from the chair and against him.

"Time for a drive."

She stamped on his foot with the heel of her shoe. His grip loosened, and she pulled from his grasp. Desperation streaked through her, and she raked her fingers across his face. She couldn't get in a car. Not with him. She turned. Sprinted down the hall. His heavy footsteps chased her. She reached the staircase. Felt him grab her upper arms. She screamed and kicked him.

"Let me go, you monster." If she screamed loud enough, maybe someone would hear. Maybe someone would call the police. He dragged her through the dining room and toward the back door. Sobs shook her. *Please rescue me.*

He scooped the rope from the table and tucked it in his pocket. Pushed the gun in her side. "Make a sound, and I end this here." His tone left no doubt he would.

Dani followed him down the steps and struggled to keep up as he pulled her across the yard. The fresh air slapped across her face. She inhaled, and her mind cleared. "Why, Phil? Help me understand."

He ignored her. Opening the door to his SUV, he shoved the gun farther into her ribs. "Climb in and slide over."

She did and reached for the passenger door. The sound of the gun cocking stopped her. A rough hand pulled her back. He grabbed the rope and flipped it around her wrists until the rope tied them together. Her attempts to flex her wrists and wiggle out of the knots failed. He ducked and placed something under the car. Sliding behind the wheel, he backed the SUV out of its slot. "Say goodbye to your house."

OSBORNE ZIPPED through traffic as Caleb called Westmont. "Tell me you have something on Dani's phone."

"It's located somewhere near her house. The unit there hasn't found it."

"Is she there?"

Westmont hesitated. "They haven't located her yet."

Pain radiated a path across Caleb's chest. The seat belt had worked too well. He pushed past the discomfort. Time was too short to chase Phil around Lincoln. And what if it wasn't Baker? *Give me wisdom, Lord.* Nothing. The heavens had turned to brass. *God, I have to hear You, or I'll go crazy with possibilities.*

Trust Me. The quiet words penetrated his soul and stilled the blood pounding in his ears.

Trust You with what? Did he really want to hear the answer?

Trust Me with this. With what is most dear to you.

Images of what the stalker would do to Dani flooded Caleb's mind. Could he trust God? Did he have a choice?

THEY DROVE ACROSS TOWN. Dani stared at each car, looking for a police officer. "What did you do with Aunt Jayne?"

"She's at your home resting comfortably in a bedroom. The police will find her when they look for you. Don't worry, she'll grieve your passing. If she remembers who you are that day."

Melancholy settled on her, even as she wanted to fight. "Why me?"

"You're one of two people who can link me to the scene of the crime."

Dani turned and looked at him. He flicked his gaze from the road to meet hers. Lucidity slipped into his expression. Somewhere in his twisted mind he believed she knew more than she did. "You know I couldn't link you. You're up to date on my investigation."

A manic chuckle filled the SUV. "And you shared everything? You're not the only one who's worked big markets. I know reporters. You're trained to hoard information. That's why I intervened. You're in this predicament because you wouldn't stop."

As he turned onto a highway, Dani realized she had no idea where they were. A manufacturing plant stood across the highway, and fields dotted the horizon.

"What will your family think when they learn what you've done?"

"They won't find out. Life will continue. I may accept a job in Kansas City, but it won't be necessary to leave." He turned left onto a side road.

Dani swallowed around a lump. How would Caleb find her? Phil drove her farther from Lincoln, and then followed a sign toward Branched Oak. A spike of hope shot through her and she sat up straighten Caleb lived somewhere near here. That would explain why she didn't remember the location. It had been ten years since she'd driven there during the day.

He turned onto a side street, and then into a pocked driveway leading to a rustic cabin. He pulled her from the SUV, dragged her up four steps into the home's rugged kitchen. Her foot slipped on a rag rug. He caught her roughly, pushed her to a bar stool. "Any last requests?"

～

THE OFFICER PULLED the car behind Dani's house. Caleb raced to the door followed by the officer. Two patrolmen met him there. "One of you head up front and cover the door."

As the officer jumped the short fence, Caleb prayed. He braced himself for whatever waited when they opened the door.

"We've searched the house. Didn't find anything." The remaining patrolman couldn't be more than twenty and looked a week out of the police academy.

"A woman could die. We're going to check again."

The officer bobbed his head.

"Good. Follow me." Caleb twisted the knob and pushed the door in.

He swept into the kitchen followed by Rookie through each room. "Up here."

Caleb raced toward the stairs, all pain forgotten. "What do you have?"

"Elderly woman, out cold, on a bed."

"Is she still breathing?" Caleb rushed into the room. Jayne was so still. He jerked to a stop next to her. Groped for her hand. Found a thready pulse. "Get an ambulance here. Now. Anyone else?"

The other policemen rushed into the room and shook their heads.

"Anyone check the basement earlier?"

"Yes, sir." Osborne nodded. "There's nothing but a bunch of boxes."

Caleb looked at the rookie who stood in the corner, eyes wide like a puppy who knows it could get stepped on. "I'm calling an ambulance and the crime scene techs. Do not leave this house until I get back or the chief tells you to clear it. Contain the scene." He slapped the guy on the shoulder. "Stay with Mrs. Richards until help arrives."

Where was Dani? His heart clenched. He was supposed to protect her. Instead, he'd failed her again.

Jayne stirred on the bed. Caleb hurried to her side. "Mrs. Richards? An ambulance is on the way. You're safe now."

"Dani? Does he have her?"

"We will find her."

"He hates her so much." Her face crumpled as if she was going to start crying.

"Where was he taking her?"

"I don't know." She tried to sit up, but collapsed. "I've always liked him. Never thought he'd be so evil. He seems so nice." Her words trailed off as she closed her eyes.

Jayne knew Dani's stalker. It was someone she'd always liked. Sounded like a public figure. Added to the tickets and the house, she'd confirmed his gut. He had to find Phil Baker. When he did, he'd find Dani.

He pointed to Osborne. "You and I are going for a ride." Caleb raced to the car, Osborne trailing. His phone rang. He glanced at the caller ID and saw Westmont's name. "Yep?" "His house is clear. Nobody there."

"Dani's not at her house, but her aunt is. Baker has a family cabin near Branched Oak. Grab Denimore and meet me there." As soon as they climbed in the car, he gave the directions to Osborne. "Get us there as fast as you can."

Caleb looked at the dashboard clock. Twenty-two hours to find Dani. Twenty-two hours.

28

Phil's voice washed over Dani, the smooth tones of a seasoned anchor shifting to menace. "I hate to bring you here. This place was a wreck when I inherited it. Now it's my haven. Renee never got to come here." He grimaced. "Can't shoot you though. Can't have a mess for someone to discover." His fingers played with the rope.

She glanced around the room. There was no escape from his twisted logic. Or his plan. Shards of pain spiked up her arms. The rope cut into her wrists. She couldn't loosen the rope's hold. Light filtering through the dirty windows flitted off the gun where it sat on the battered table in front of him.

Her gaze whipped from him to the gun. Would he strangle her like he'd strangled Renee? Her body quaked. Somewhere in his demented mind he'd decided she had to go. He twirled the rope through his fingers.

She should have known. Pieces clicked into place, making her question her investigative abilities. She'd been so close to the truth but distracted.

Dani shuddered at the emptiness in his eyes.

He stood and picked up the rope. "It's time."

"Let me tell you what I think Renee did." She had to keep talking. Had to buy time for Caleb to find her. He stepped closer.

"Turn here."

Osborne spun the steering wheel at Caleb's barked direction.

"The cabin should be on the left. Slow down. We can't miss it."

The car crawled down the road. Caleb wanted to find the cabin and pound the door. His thoughts jumbled. *Lord, keep Dani alive. I've failed her so many times. But You never have. Be her rescuer.* He scanned one side of the street and then the other. His vision began to blur, and he shook his head. She could die if he missed the cabin. Every minute counted.

"There. That's it." He unstrapped the seat belt and leaped from the car before Osborne threw it into Park.

Osborne hopped out of the car, hand on his gun.

"Wait." Caleb's words commanded obedience. "You've got to stay with me." He took in the environment. Cabins crowded small lots. A street ran between the rows. The cabins looked empty, no one around to get caught in the middle. He itched to join Osborne in storming the cabin.

If Dani was inside... He couldn't bear to leave her alone another minute. But if Baker anticipated them coming... Caleb needed a plan and backup. "We wait for Westmont and Denimore."

Osborne rolled his eyes. "I didn't become an officer to let someone die. Especially while I stand outside. Need a body on the front stoop? Will that get you moving?"

"Don't make me cuff you and put you in the car." Caleb stood with his knees softly bent, his hands flexing open and closed. He didn't want to take the kid down. They couldn't act without thinking. That would kill Dani...if she was still alive. "It's more productive to wait sixty seconds than fight, but it's your choice."

Osborne shrugged and stepped back.

An unmarked car slid to the curb, lights flashing without sirens.

As Denimore and Westmont hustled out of the car, Caleb glanced at the kid.

"I know," Osborne said, "that wasn't long."

"Denimore," Caleb barked, "you and Westmont slip around back. We'll give you sixty seconds to get there, then we're going in. Don't let him escape."

Westmont patted his gut. "You think he's going to get past this hunk of athleticism?"

Denimore rolled his eyes, and grabbed Westmont's elbow. "Come on, marathon man."

As they slipped up the driveway, Osborne shook his head. "Those two are straight out of the *Odd Couple.*"

"Yep. but effective." He took a deep breath. Focused the adrenaline.

Caleb walked up the sidewalk and took the stairs two at a time. Osborne followed, staying a step behind.

He slowly counted to sixty. Westmont and Denimore had to be in position. Caleb waited another thirty seconds. He took a deep breath, then straightened.

DANI STOPPED midsentence when a pounding rattled the front door. Could it be? A surge of giddy relief shot through her. It didn't matter who it was. It was a distraction. "Expecting company?"

Phil stood and headed toward the door. Halfway there he stopped and turned back to her. He approached the windows in the breakfast nook and swept the curtains aside. His smooth motions turned choppy. He grabbed the rope and jerked Dani from her seat. "Come with me."

Pain seared her shoulder as he yanked her up. She twisted and tried to find an angle that didn't pull it from its socket.

When they reached the door, he threw her to the floor and trained his gun on her. "Move, and I'll shoot. Scream, and you're dead."

As he scowled at her, she clamped her lips tight over the scream creeping up her throat. She'd find another way to escape. Phil slid aside the dusty curtain covering the window next to the door and looked around the porch.

"Come." He pulled her off the floor and back toward the kitchen, but detoured into a bedroom. After pushing her onto a twin bed that groaned in protest, he stalked to the window. Dani craned her neck to look out the window.

Caleb and a uniformed officer huddled on the front steps. The cavalry had arrived. She had to give them time to get inside.

Phil stayed glued to the window. Sweat streaked his face. Her heart pounded a rapid beat. This was her chance. She slid to the edge of the bed, cringing when it squealed. Snuck a glance at him, but he hadn't noticed. She eased off and rushed toward the door. An icy hand grabbed her. Yanked her against him.

"You're not going anywhere."

His heartbeat thundered in her ears. Drowned out the pounding in her chest. Thoughts of escape evaporated when he pushed his gun into her neck.

"I told you not to try anything. I don't care who's here." The words slithered into her ear.

This is it. There was so much she wouldn't do. She'd never be there, waiting, when her daughter searched for her. She'd never build a future with Caleb. And she'd never walk Aunt Jayne through her disease. Instead, she'd leave the house in a body bag. *God, I'm not ready to die. But if I do, forgive me for walking away from You.* She thought she'd hyperventilate. The gun never strayed. She gulped against its hardness.

"WHY AREN'T WE DOING SOMETHING?" Osborne whispered the words in Caleb's ear.

Caleb waved him back and pounded the door again. A bead of sweat trickled between his shoulder blades. Dani had to be here. He couldn't fail her again. The cost was too high. He shook his head and turned to the door. A curtain fluttered in the window next to the door.

Phil looked around the curtain. Caleb's muscles bunched. Phil could choke the life from her even now. Showtime.

"Police, open now."

DANI MOANED when she heard his voice. Caleb was trying. He was a good man, and she'd never get to tell him. Phil dropped his hold on her arm but kept the gun jammed against her throat. She felt him reach into his pocket. Closed her eyes as he brushed her hair back from her neck. The nylon rope slid around her throat.

Her mind raced. Had it been a week since he killed Renee? Had he made Renee anticipate her death? Fear disappeared in the light of Dani's intense desire to live. She flailed against him. Clutched at the rope as it tightened. The more she struggled the tighter he pulled.

The rope cut into her airway. She tried to slip her fingers under it. Tried to find any space to breathe. Her vision spotted. She rose on tiptoe against the pull. Nothing worked. She groped for the gun. He batted her hand away. She grabbed again. With her last strength, she stomped her heel onto his foot. Connected with the gun. Pulled it away when he loosened his grip. She clicked the safety off and pointed behind her. Fired the gun.

She jumped at the gun's report. Phil's grip tightened then loosened. Slightly. Just enough to breathe. She gulped air as he yanked back on the cord.

Distantly she heard the splinter of wood, followed by a louder, closer crash. Feet pounded down the hall.

"God, save me," she whispered. Peace settled on her.

She'd fought as hard as she could.

Phil had won.

She slipped into darkness.

～

WHEN THE BULLET FIRED, Caleb lunged against the door with more force than he'd ever used, breaking it open. Osborne raced around the corner and rammed into Caleb. Caleb pushed him aside, and heard a clunk after a gun slipped from Dani's fingers to the floor.

Dani hung like a ragdoll against Phil's grasp. She was so still. Westmont bolted through the door and threw himself against Phil's knees. Phil fell to the floor, and Westmont hung on.

Caleb slapped handcuffs on Phil and tossed him on the bed. He pulled Dani into his arms, cradled her against him. An angry red line laced her throat.

"Lord, please no."

He watched, praying her chest would lift.

Phil laughed as Westmont pulled him up.

"You can't have her," he spat. "You're too late."

Denimore rushed in and helped Westmont with Baker.

"We'll get him back to the station. This time we'll even take his picture and fingerprint him." Yanking Phil toward the door, Westmont hustled him out of the room.

Osborne talked into his radio. "An ambulance is on the way."

"She's still breathing." Caleb examined Dani carefully, praying that her chest would keep rising. Over and over again. Until the paramedics arrived. "I almost lost her."

He held Dani in his arms. EMTs rushed in, removed her and strapped her to a gurney. They wheeled her from the building.

He hung his head after they took her, drained. A ragged breath dragged from him. Holding her, all he'd wanted was to promise her forever. Would he have that chance? Ask for her forgiveness for the past? Would she forgive him? Walk with him into the future?

The ambulance tore down the street, sirens blaring.

29

D ani touched the rough line on her throat. She still couldn't believe she was back at Aunt Jayne's. When she'd regained consciousness in the hospital, Caleb had been slumped in a chair next to her bed. He'd rarely left her side until the doctors discharged her the next day.

Her first thought had been about Aunt Jayne. Caleb quickly settled her fears and reassured her Aunt Jayne would be fine. He'd helped her walk down the hall to her aunt's room. Tears had slipped down her cheeks as she watched the older woman sleep.

Dani shifted on her sofa, grateful she'd only spent one night in the hospital before talking her way home. She pulled a quilt over her legs and flipped on the TV. Kate had graciously given her four days to recover—two happened to fall on the weekend.

That first day back would be hard. How would everyone respond to her? To the knowledge she'd helped destroy the station's star? Someday she hoped to understand why Phil had killed Renee. It seemed like a straightforward case of twisted love and jealousy. Renee had pushed Phil too far. She'd flirted with him, gotten the house and then lost interest. His ego couldn't handle the challenge. When she took Reed Donovan to the theater, Phil had imploded. But why give up his family and career? How would killing Renee solve anything? She pulled the quilt higher to ward off a sudden chill.

Reed had finally stepped forward, now that he was clear of murder charges. He'd have to fight obstruction of justice charges though.

Dani picked up the latest edition of *Newsweek* and flipped through it. She was already bored. After the last week, she should want nothing more than to relax, but she was ready to tackle the world. She'd just wear turtlenecks for a while.

From her perch, she could read part of the words scrolled on the dining room wall. *Find rest, O my soul, in God alone.* A longing to rediscover a friendship with God filled her every time she read them.

She gently rubbed the line again. During the last week, Phil had exposed every fear she had. She'd come so close to death. But God had used the week to expose her need for Him. And to expose her need to move beyond the past. God had saved her from Phil and so much more. Now, she'd relearn that He saw her and that He cared.

A knock on the door interrupted her thoughts. She shifted on the couch and pulled the lace curtain to the side. A smile tipped her lips as she looked out the window. Caleb stood on the porch, a Valentino's box in his hand. She could almost smell the fresh pizza.

She rapped on the window and motioned him to enter. As he slipped through the door, she heard the scratch of nails slipping on the wood floors. A moment later, a wet nose pressed against her cheek.

"Job! Where did you find him?" Dani asked.

"Tricia and I called around and finally found him at the shelter."

"It's so good to have you back, boy."

As she watched Caleb settle next to her, Dani smiled.

"That smells great."

"I brought your favorite." He leaned in and stroked her cheek with a soft touch. She stilled as his eyes filled with tears. "I almost lost you. There's so much I haven't said.

"Dani, you are a treasure. Can you forgive me for walking away instead of fighting for you? Fighting for us? I didn't understand what I was doing." He paused. "No, that's not true. I knew, but was too young to care. Now I know what I want, and I will fight for you."

She placed a finger on his lips. "You already have. I forgive you." She shuddered. "Will you forgive me for not letting you know about our baby?"

He searched her face, and her fingers clutched the edges of the blanket. Her heart sank. He couldn't do it, and she couldn't blame him. She could hardly forgive herself for not fighting for her baby girl. She looked away and tried to ignore the emotional connection between them.

"Don't do it, Dani. Don't pull away from me already."

Her eyes lifted to the verse in the other room.

Caleb tipped her chin, his thumb casually running along her jaw. Dani trembled.

"It's time to stop living with regrets. Ten years ago, I wouldn't have fought for the baby any more than I fought for you. I would have been relieved to not deal with the responsibility. So, yes, I forgive you. But only if you'll accept that I am different today."

The last week replayed through Dani's mind.

In each instance he'd proven he was a fighter. For her. For justice. For Aunt Jayne. Not once had he shown a flash of the boy she'd been infatuated with.

He hadn't stolen her heart this week.

No, he'd earned the right to request it.

"I'm ready to move out of the shadows of our past." Caleb's look smoldered, and Dani swallowed. Hard. His lips brushed her forehead, and she closed her eyes. Savoring the feel of his touch, but afraid of what could happen.

She cleared her throat, and he pulled away.

"Dani, I want a relationship with you, but I want it the right way this time. Will you move into the future with me? Explore what it holds?"

She opened her eyes and studied his face. She knew to the very core of her being that Caleb was the man for her. If they could do this right... Warmth surged through her. They could do this. They didn't have to be trapped by their past or condemned to repeat it. A slow smile spread across his face and into his eyes.

Dani frowned and pulled her hand from his. "What?" "You're so cute. Your emotions flash across your face." "Then I guess I don't have to answer your question." "No." He grabbed her hand and kissed the palm before pulling her close. "So does this mean I get Job?"

She quirked an eyebrow at him. "Um. No. He's mine." "And you're mine. So that makes him mine, too."

She turned to look at him. He leaned toward her, and she waited. Her eyes closed as his lips touched her. In that moment, she knew.

The nightmare was behind her.

Today was filled with the promise of new beginnings. And the best beginning included the man in front of her. The man who had worked so hard to protect her. And who loved her with an intensity that blinded her. Dani smiled, eager to walk into the future with Caleb by her side.

TRIAL BY FIRE

Chapter One

Thursday, Lincoln, Nebraska

Another broken dream rested in front of Deputy County Attorney Tricia Jamison.

The phone ringing on the desk pulled her thoughts from the file. She glanced at her watch. The afternoon had evaporated while she flipped through new case files and absorbed the dashed hopes each one represented. She'd taken the job because she wanted to help people, those who didn't have anyone to protect them. Each time she got a new file, she had the opportunity to make a difference for a family. She'd seen God heal families when directed to the right resources. But every time another domestic violence case crossed her desk it was hard not to grow discouraged. Too many times the hope of happily-ever-afters had gone horribly wrong. She shook her head and grabbed the still ringing phone.

"Tricia Jamison, deputy prosecutor."

"Trish, this is Caleb. There's a fire at Mom's." Her brother's voice had an edge of tension she hadn't heard in a while. As a police investigator, he usually kept his emotions tightly controlled. She hadn't heard him sound so rattled since last year when a stalker set his sights on Caleb's girlfriend, Dani Richard. Her breath caught in her chest as she shut the file on her desk. "How bad?"

"Don't know. I heard it on my scanner before Mom called."

"Is she safe?"

There was a pause, then a sigh. "Yes."

"I'm leaving now." Her jaw clenched. Images of flames lapping at her mother's home raced through her mind. The home encapsulated so many memories, both good and bad.

Tricia grabbed her purse and keys, and ran toward the elevator. She slid to a stop at her paralegal's desk. "Family emergency. I'll be back tomorrow."

"I'll cover for you." The woman leaned back in her chair, a concerned expression on her face.

"Thanks." Tricia jogged the rest of the way to the elevator. She punched the down button and paced until the doors opened.

Twenty minutes later she'd crossed town and pulled into her mom's neighborhood. Flashing lights drew her toward the small ranch home. She parked several houses down, and rushed to join Caleb and Mom in the neighbor's yard. Caleb had his arm around their mother's shoulders, and she'd sunk against his side, an unusual posture for one who liked to stand firmly on her own two feet. The heavy smell of smoke curled through the air, but no matter how Tricia squinted against the western sun, the house looked intact. In fact, there weren't many firefighters in the front yard.

"Are you okay?"

The petite woman tipped her chin up, brown eyes flashing. "Of course. Some kid decided the garage made a good fire-starter."

"Where's Frank?" Tricia's stepfather usually rushed to his wife's side anytime she whimpered or looked a little cross. Tricia couldn't fault his devotion to her mom.

"At work. He wanted to come home, but I told him not to hurry. It's a small fire." A tremble in Mom's voice belied her strong front.

"From Caleb's call I thought the flames had engulfed the house."

Mom poked him in the ribs. "I told you not to make a big deal."

"A fire is never small." He rubbed his side with a frown. "The wind blows in the wrong direction, and the outcome could change. It almost reached the house."

"But it didn't. Relax." There was still a tightness at the corner of her eyes even as Mom forced a smile.

"Sure." Caleb grimaced over her head at Tricia. "We'll never worry about you when panic fills your voice. Fires are everyday occurrences."

"You can't protect everyone." Even as she said the words, Tricia knew he wouldn't accept them.

"You believe that?" He rolled his eyes. "Sure. That's why you're a prosecutor."

"Someone has to do it." Tricia grinned at him. She'd had a life-time to perfect the art of poking his weak spots. Tell Caleb he couldn't take care of everyone, and he bristled like a porcupine. Good thing she was a pro at sidestepping his quills.

"All right, you two. You can bicker all you want inside. I want to get out of this yard before we trample the Johnsons' grass. You know how fastidious George is." Mom tugged Caleb's sleeve until he joined her.

A couple of firefighters turned the corner from the backyard into the front. One pulled off his helmet and ran a hand through smooshed hair, sweat streaking his face. He caught Tricia's glance and grimaced. Her heart stopped, and she took a shuddering breath. Noah Brust. In the flesh, and looking even better in his turnout coat with soot on his face than he had the last time she'd seen him in the courtroom.

"Mrs. Randol?" His voice was low, with a rich timbre to it. It tickled her senses, and her stomach tightened, even though the man ignored her.

"Yes," her mother answered.

"I'm Noah Brust with the Lincoln Fire Department. We've contained the fire. The shed will be a total loss, but we kept it from the house."

Mom put a trembling hand to her mouth, then nodded. "Thank

you. We'll replace the things in the shed. Frank will probably enjoy the excuse to buy more tools."

"Investigator Caleb Jamison, LPD." Caleb extended his hand, and the firefighter shook it. "This is my sister, Tricia Jamison."

Noah turned a blank expression her way. "We've met."

Tricia nodded, searching for a hint of emotion on his face. Even anger seemed better than the nothingness he registered when looking at her. Instead, he wore a look of schooled indifference. This from the rugged fireman who'd almost swept her off her feet when she'd prepped him for his testimony during the Lincoln Life fire trial a year before. Despite the attraction that zinged between them, he'd made it clear at the close of his testimony that he wanted nothing to do with her.

She stifled the urge to grab his collar and force him to acknowledge her. Mom threw her a questioning look, and Tricia shook her head. Now was not the time to explain.

"Any clues on how the fire started?" Caleb pulled her attention back to the fire.

Noah focused on Caleb. "The captain will likely call in the fire investigation team. Until they work their magic I can guess at a cause, but that's it. We'll keep an eye on the fire while we clean up. We'll leave only when we're sure the fire's out, but it's safe to go inside your home now."

"Thank you." Mom pulled the collar of her jacket tight around her throat against the October wind as she hurried toward the house.

Heat climbed Tricia's face, and she turned to find Noah watching her. "Thanks for helping Mom."

"You're welcome."

She fought the urge to rub her arms, try to generate some warmth against the chill emanating from him. "You're still angry about the Lincoln Life case? I did everything the law allowed."

His blue eyes, which had so captured her attention before, had frosted over. Noah snorted and shook his head. "Thanks to you, I read a dozen articles accusing my father—one of the best firefighters I've ever known—of negligence in his duties." His voice rose with each word. "He died a hero, but you didn't raise a finger to stop them from slandering him at the trial."

She looked around for a way to escape the barrage of angry words. "I'm sorry you don't appreciate the rules of court and their limitations. And don't forget, we won." Tricia turned at the sound of more cars pulling into the cul-de-sac. The Channel 13 Jeep jerked into park as Caleb reappeared at her shoulder.

"You okay, sis?" Caleb furrowed his brow until the eyebrows merged.

"Fine. I'll be there in a minute, Caleb." She turned to Firefighter Brust and twisted her lips into what she hoped passed for a smile. "I'm sorry I couldn't do more to protect you and your father. Now, if you don't want to create another scene worthy of the papers, let me pass. The media have arrived." She tipped her chin, pushed past him and marched to Caleb's side. "Let's go inside now, please."

Tricia refused to look back as Caleb hurried her into the house. She tried to ignore the tremble in her limbs when she sat on the couch next to her mother.

"Anything you need to tell me?" Caleb stood in front of her in full big brother mode.

"An unpleasant reminder of a case from last year."

"Looked like more."

"No." Tricia shook her head. "He thinks I didn't do my job. There's nothing I can do to change his mind. If I'm lucky, I won't run into him again."

Today had been a fluke. That's all.

Then why did the pain hiding in his cold eyes cut so?

Noah watched the media park on the cul-de-sac. He stood straight and prepared for the onslaught. "The vultures descend."

Graham Jackson groaned and yanked his helmet off. "Come on, man. Hold it together."

"You're right." Noah frowned and ran a hand over his face. Some days he felt so tired, he wondered how long he'd keep up with the job. Fighting through the lingering impact of the knee he'd injured in the Lincoln Life fire seemed impossible. He tried to hide it on the job, but rarely succeeded. "So, I lost my composure."

"Yep." Graham climbed onto the fire truck, tossing his helmet onto the seat next to him. He grabbed two bottles of water and tossed one to Noah. "Fortunately, the press arrived late and didn't see your show. What was that all about, anyway? I've never seen you that worked up around a woman." Noah unscrewed the lid and sat opposite Graham. He forced the image of Tricia's face from his mind. She looked as beautiful as she had when he'd met her the year before. He'd been instantly smitten with the spunky lawyer...but couldn't let himself think about that now. Not after the way she'd let him down. "Hope you're right about the media." He swiped the cool bottle against his forehead, ignoring Graham's stare. "I keep waiting for it to get easier. You'd think it would after a year."

"You still haven't answered my question."

"She was the attorney on the Lincoln Life case."

Graham looked toward the house. "She's cute."

"I'd hoped she was more." Much more. "But I was wrong."

"Don't push so hard. This was a simple outbuilding fire, and you barked orders like flames were engulfing the Cornhusker Hotel."

"I acted crazy. She brings that out in me." Noah ran his fingers through his hair and grimaced.

"No. A little overzealous, but it's okay. Temper it. That's all I'm saying."

An hour later, the firefighters cleared the scene and headed back to the fire station. The rest of the shift dragged as Noah tried to focus on the paperwork in front of him, rather than Tricia Jamison.

That night, long after he should have been asleep, Noah lay in bed and couldn't stop thinking about the prosecutor and the trial. Before he'd taken the stand, he'd had a dinner invitation planned for Tricia. Test the sparks between them. Then she'd let him down during what she'd said would be an easy cross-examination. He forced the memory from his mind, but thoughts of his father's death marched into its place.

His chest tightened at the flashback of how close he'd gotten to saving his father, but not close enough. When the ceiling collapsed between them, he'd known he'd failed. Waited too long. Tried too hard to save everybody else. Failed to save his father's life.

Thanks to Tricia Jamison, he hadn't salvaged the man's reputation, either. That he couldn't forgive. No matter how beautiful she looked.

Intrigued? Want to read the rest of Tricia's story in Trial by Fire? *Then click here to order it from your favorite retailer.*

DON'T MISS THE BOOK THAT
USA TODAY BESTSELLING AUTHOR
COLLEEN COBLE CALLED
"SPECTACULAR"!

THOMAS NELSON
Since 1798

AVAILABLE IN PRINT AND E-BOOK APRIL 2017!

BEYOND JUSTICE EXCERPT

PROLOGUE

JANUARY

If he didn't find that flash drive now, he would have to disappear. Immediately.

Some place el jefe couldn't find him. It was that or die.

"Where is it, Miguel? What have you done with the information you stole?"

The young man shuddered as he choked on a breath. Blood poured from his nose, broken in the first punch, the horror of it fresh. Blood dribbled out his mouth. Blood dripped off his chin. Still he refused to speak.

Rafael drew back his fist, ready to strike again, then held his arm back as if against a powerful force. This was not who he was. It was not who Miguel was. All of this was so broken. Somehow he had landed on the wrong side of the great family his own had served for three generations.

How was he now opposing the young man he loved like a brother? He scanned the bare room. Four bunk beds lined a wall. A urinal in the corner. A barren sink with a square mirror. A single light bulb hanging well above his head. Where could Miguel have hidden anything in this desolate place?

The stench of urine and sweat, of bodies crammed into a space designed for half as many, mixed with the coppery aroma of fresh blood.

Limp sunlight pushed back the shadows from a barred window high on the wall. Sunlight that reminded him of the times Miguel had tagged along when Rafael did odd chores at the estate. Sunlight that reminded him how wrong it was for Miguel to be here. He was the son of a lord, not someone who should be locked up.

"Where is it, Miguel? I can't ask again." He flipped open the blade of the knife he held and slid it under Miguel's chin. "Give it to me, or I have no choice but to kill you."

Miguel flinched. "We always have a choice." The youth lifted his chin and met Rafael's gaze with pain-filled eyes. "We are brothers, Rafael."

"We were. If you don't give me that flash drive, we are both dead."

"I don't know what you're talking about."

"Liar! El jefe knows you were in his computer. He told me himself. He sent me."

"You kill me, and my father will hunt you like a rabid mongrel." False bravado flashed in Miguel's eyes.

"Your father told me to kill you, amigo."

The spoken words resounded in the narrow space between them. He looked at señor's precious son. His heir. Could he somehow take Miguel with him and disappear? No. Would Miguel give him the list? The boy raised dark eyes to meet his gaze, defiance hardening them. Somehow Rafael had imagined he could avoid killing while serving the family even as he'd crept up its structure. But now he had no choice.

Retrieve the information for el jefe before it falls into the wrong hands or be killed.

Heat flooded him and red clouded his vision.

"I'm sorry, Miguel . . ." He stepped forward, knife clasped in his fist.

~

CHAPTER ONE

THURSDAY, MARCH 30

The euphoria of winning a hard case vied in her thoughts with wondering what came next as Hayden McCarthy left the Alexandria courthouse. A colorful dance of tulips lined a flower box of the town house across the street, and the faint aroma of some hidden blossom scented the air. It was over.

Her client had needed her absolute best. Hayden had delivered it and obtained justice. She shifted her purse and readjusted her brief-case as she started down the street. Continue straight on King Street, and in a block she'd be at the office. Turn, and in four blocks she'd be home. Her town house's proximity both to work and the heart of Old Town Alexandria was why she loved the space she shared with a friend from law school.

So . . . which way to go? The thought of going back to her office and confronting the waiting pile of work held no appeal. She would spend one night savoring success . . . and recovering from the adrenaline pace of a roller-coaster trial and jury.

She'd make a salad and cup of tea, maybe pick up a novel. If that didn't hold her attention, she'd dig into her trial notes. Analyze what had worked and how the risk of requesting a new foreman after deliberations had begun had paid off.

Each step closer to home, her conservative navy pumps tapped the refrain. She. Had. Won. She let a smile spread across her face.

She left King Street and headed north on St. Asaph. Some of the buildings she passed housed businesses, but with each block the area became more residential. In one condo a senator lived. In another a congressman, next to him a chief of staff and other people with powerful political positions. When Hayden first moved to the city from small-town Nebraska, her head had turned at how easy it was to rub elbows with those who controlled destinies. Now it was only scandals or surprise retirements that caught her attention.

The evening was so pleasant she detoured and walked the couple blocks to Christ Church. The wrought iron fence around the church grounds beckoned her to settle in the shade of the stately trees. She opened the gate, then walked until she reached a bench. Settling on it, she breathed deeply and closed her eyes.

Father, thank You. It went well today. She pushed against her eyes, daring relieved tears to fall. There was no one else around, and Hayden sat quietly, waiting . . . for something. Here within the shelter of a church more than two hundred years old, shouldn't she feel God's presence?

Yet there was . . . nothing.

Not even a rustle of a breeze through the leaves that she could pretend was the Spirit moving.

I need You.

Still nothing. Then slowly she sensed His smile as warmth spread through her.

A couple came around the corner then, strolling along the garden path arm in arm, smiling at one another. They looked at ease and in tune as their strides matched.

What would it feel like to be that comfortable and safe with someone? To know you could trust another person with your most hidden parts? Hayden shook her head. Her life was full to the brim— no room for a relationship. She stood and walked the rest of the way home at a brisk pace.

When she reached her town house, she crossed the courtyard and dug her keys loose from the pit of her purse. The Wonder Woman keyring, a gift from a grateful client after she won what he called the unwinnable case, jiggled as she unlocked the door.

The moment she walked inside, Hayden kicked off her heels and set her bag on the chair next to the glass table by the door. Soft classical music flowed from the kitchen, and the aroma of something spicy filled the small space.

"Emilie?" Hayden leaned down to rub one of her arches, then straightened and moved toward the kitchen.

"Down here." Emilie Wesley's bubbly voice came from the stairway leading to the basement. "Can you check the oven for me?"

"Sure. What are you making?" Hayden moved around the granite countertop and turned on the oven light. Emilie was a wonderful cook, but she often got distracted. "Mmm, lasagna. Looks great. It's bubbling around the edges, and the cheese looks perfect. You expecting company?"

Hayden opened the fridge and pulled out salad ingredients. A salad plus a glass of sweet tea and she could disappear into her room . . .though the pasta looked wonderful. If she was lucky, Emilie would save her some for lunch tomorrow.

Hayden was dicing a red pepper when two sets of footsteps echoed up the stairs.

"Look who stopped by, Hayden."

"Hmm?" Hayden looked up and into clear blue eyes that matched the Potomac as it moved into the bay. His pressed khakis and Oxford with pullover sweater portrayed an understated GQ elegance that screamed old money and matched the clean haircut and polite smile that revealed teeth so perfect they might be caps. Andrew Wesley, her roommate's cousin. She hadn't seen him in years.

The knife slipped, and she felt a sharp pain in her finger. She turned on the tap and stuck her finger beneath the flow of cold water.

"Andrew, do you remember my roommate, Hayden McCarthy? Hayden, this is my cousin Andrew. It's been a while, but I'm pretty sure y'all have met before." Emilie's eyes danced as she tugged the man into the room. His mouth curved into a relaxed grin, the look as familiar and practiced as Hayden's in court.

The years had been good to Andrew Wesley. He'd been handsome when they'd first met, but now he was something more. He had the build of someone who worked out and took care of himself. Compact, muscular, and distractingly good-looking. Hayden pasted a smile into place.

"Hayden?" The deep voice was thick as the richest chocolate. "It's nice to officially meet you—again." He gave her a devastating smile.

"Emilie is always talking about you."

"Good things, I hope." She grabbed a paper towel and turned off the water.

"What else would I say?" Emilie's eyes widened as she saw blood seeping through the paper towel. "Ooh, do you need a Band-Aid?"

"I'll be all right." Hayden took a deep breath and met Andrew's gaze.

"Any friend—or cousin—of Emilie's is welcome here." With her good hand she scooped up the diced pepper and sprinkled it on top of the salad. "I'll leave you two to enjoy your dinner. It looks good, Em."

"You don't need to leave, Hayden." Emilie leaned closer, not hard to do in the galley space that felt even smaller with Andrew's presence, and handed Hayden a fresh paper towel. "We're working on plans for a spring festival. Think inflatables, fair food, and fun. It's a community event for his non-profit." She grabbed a purple grape from a bowl next to the sink and popped it into her mouth. "You can help us."

His cousin's roommate wrapped the paper towel tighter around her finger, then turned to the refrigerator, shielding her face from his view.

Had they really met before? He had a vague recollection of an awkward girl visiting his cousin during a law school break, but his memory didn't match this attractive woman with the black hair and .. . stocking feet.

As Hayden put away the vegetables she'd used for her salad, Andrew looked for something to break the uncomfortable silence.

"I like the idea of a festival, Em, but I'm not sure we can pull it off."

"Oh? You already have the location." Emilie claimed the pot holders and opened the oven. "We can do this because we're the dynamic duo. Besides, you've got a staff and board of directors to help. We'll create the framework, and they can do the rest."

Andrew shook his head. "You haven't worked much with a board. And don't forget, I'm not the senior guy in the office."

Emilie slid the pan from the oven and set it on top of the stove.

"You're a Wesley. Everyone takes one look at you and snaps to attention. Your dad is too powerful to tick off." She softened the words with a smile. "You might as well embrace it."

That was something that hadn't happened yet in his thirty years. Being Scott Wesley's son was like wearing a coat made for someone else.

He leaned against the counter and redirected the conversation—a skill he'd picked up from his father. "I've heard about Emilie's day, Hayden. Tell me about yours."

Hayden paused, salad dressing in hand. "I won a case today."

"Oh?" He studied her face, but she didn't give anything away. Not much of a talker?

She shrugged. "I kept an innocent man out of jail. So it was a great day for my client and his wife."

"For you too." Emilie stepped next to Hayden and squeezed her shoulder. "This woman worked a lot of late nights on that case and is on the fast track to becoming a partner." Hayden started to protest, but Emilie kept on. "She'll never brag about herself, but she's good. Nobody will be surprised when she becomes the youngest partner in Elliott & Johnson history."

Soft color tinted the woman's cheeks, and she glanced at Andrew. "I'm not any better than a hundred other attorneys in town."

Only a hundred, huh? In a city overwhelmed with attorneys, she'd ranked herself fairly high. Well, the last thing he wanted to do was spend free time with an attorney. He'd spent too much time in their presence growing up to be wowed by their brilliance or awed by their stories.

She held up her salad bowl and fork. "I know y'all have plans to make, so I'll slip upstairs and not interrupt. It was nice to see you again, Andrew."

Andrew put a hand on her arm before she could disappear. "You really want to walk away from Emilie's lasagna for that?" He crinkled his nose and pointed at the bowl of greens.

Emilie grabbed an extra plate. "There's plenty, Hayden."

Andrew grinned. "Always is. She forgets there's only two of us."

He said it as though these evenings were frequent, but they weren't.

Emilie was as busy as anyone in town, so he'd pounced on her invitation. When they all sat down at the island a few minutes later, he watched Hayden. She looked tired. A good trial would do that, his dad always said. He and Emilie kept a quiet conversation going, with Hayden interjecting now and then.

She'd made it through law school, and he admired anyone who did that. He'd quit after a semester—but that had more to do with wanting to become his own man rather than an ever-lengthening part of his father's shadow.

A phone beeped, and Hayden glanced at hers and frowned. "Sorry, but I need to prepare for a meeting in the morning. Nice to see you, Andrew." She stood and brushed past him with a small smile.

He watched her cross the living space and head toward the stairs. As she climbed from view he reminded himself that he didn't have time to feel attracted to anyone right now. Not when Congressman Wesley was gunning for a title change. Anyone he was seen with would end up plastered across the social pages of the Post the next day. Who would willingly sign up for that?

He turned back to the kitchen and found Emilie smirking at him.

"I'm not sure you're her type, Andrew." Her smile widened until her dimples showed.

He made a face at her. "Don't think I don't see right through you. I know why you had me meet you here." He was just surprised it had taken this long. "It doesn't matter. I'm too busy to get involved right now."

BUY NOW.

Don't miss any of the books in the thrilling Hidden Justice series!

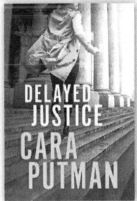

DEAR READER,

Thank you so much for joining me in Dani and Caleb's story.

I can really relate to Dani. Love often pushes us to face choices like Dani's. She could choose to live in the past, with all its hurts, disappointments and fears. Or she could move into the future and risk everything for love. It's when we risk that we give God the greatest opportunity to work in ways we couldn't imagine. Like Dani, we can find healing when we step forward and offer our hurts to Him.

Dani also had to learn that there is a point where only God can rescue us. She was about as isolated as someone can be. The only person she could turn to was a man she had every reason to hate and not trust. Even he couldn't be with her when the stalker chased her down.

But the psalmist says in Psalm 62, God alone is our fortress. And when we rely on Him, we will not be shaken. When the storms of life blow, I take great comfort in that promise.

I hope you enjoyed this journey!

QUESTIONS FOR DISCUSSION

1. Dani finds herself in a new town with the hard work of forming new friendships. Have you ever found yourself making a similar adjustment to a new city? What helped you build new friendships?

2. Dani had fallen away from God when life took an unexpected turn. How do you encourage someone in her shoes that God is trustworthy and still cares about them, despite the circumstances?

3. In what way have you ever felt abandoned by God or your family? What did you do about it?

4. Job brought joy and comfort to Dani as she struggled with the shadows chasing her. How have pets helped you during life's hard times?

5. Caleb had to learn to surrender his greatest treasure to God. Has God ever asked you to do the same? How has He proven trustworthy?

6. Dani hid her pregnancy from Caleb and denied him the opportunity to be part of the decision-making process. Have you ever hidden a decision from someone who

should have been part of it? How has that affected your life?

7. Maybe you're in Caleb's shoes and someone's hidden a life-changing event from you. Have you been able to forgive that person? How were you able to do that?

8. Caleb regrets forcing Dani into a physical relationship. Ten years later he still feels immense guilt over his actions. He knows God has forgiven him, but finds it impossible to forgive himself. What would you tell someone in his situation?

9. Is Caleb right? Are there truly sins that God's grace does not cover? Why or why not?

10. Life all too often erupts into a crisis, though fortunately for most of us, ours don't typically involve a stalker. When you've been in a crisis have you felt closer to or further away from God? Why?

11. I often find that in the middle of a crisis, I am pushed to test my faith. I discover what I really believe when my talk meets the road of real life. How has God used crises to build your faith?

12. In the end Dani opens her heart to risk a relationship with Caleb. Have you been in a similar situation? If so, what did you learn through the process?

ABOUT THE AUTHOR

Cara C. Putman, JD MBA, the award-winning author of 35 books, graduated high school at 16, college at 20, and completed her law degree at 27. FIRST for Women magazine called Shadowed by Grace "captivating" and a "novel with 'the works.'" Beyond Justice is being called a page-turner that can't be put down.

Cara is active at her church and a full-time lecturer on business and employment law to graduate students at Purdue University's Krannert School of Management. Putman also practices law and is a second-generation homeschooling mom. She serves on the executive board of American Christian Fiction Writers (ACFW), an organization she has served in various roles since 2007. She lives with her husband and four children in Indiana.

Connect with Cara and read first chapters of her books on her website: Http://caraputman.com/books.

ALSO BY CARA PUTMAN

WWII Historical Romances

Canteen Dreams

Captive Dreams

A Promise Forged

A Promise Born

A Promise Kept

Cornhusker Dreams

Buckeye Promises

WWII Romantic Mysteries

Shadowed by Grace

Stars in the Night

Legal Thrillers

Beyond Justice

Imperfect Justice

Delayed Justice

Flight Risk

Lethal Intent

Romantic Suspense

Deadly Secrets on Mackinac Island

Dying for Love, novella prequel to *Beyond Justice*

Hidden Love, novella

Trial By Fire, book 2 in Hometown Heroes

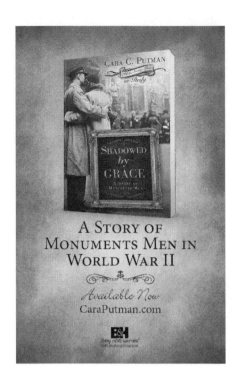

A STORY OF MONUMENTS MEN IN WORLD WAR II

Available Now
CaraPutman.com

DEADLY EXPOSURE

Cover design by Suzanne Wesley

Cover photography by stock_colors, © zef art, © Ruben, © Aldeca Productions, and © pink candy

Printed in U.S.A.

Made in the USA
Middletown, DE
29 October 2021